"I can't let you walk into a potential hostage situation. Having you there might even make the kidnappers less likely to cooperate."

She continued dressing. "I'm going with you."

"Michelle, look at me."

She glared at him. "He's my baby. He needs me. I need him."

"Yes, but I need you to stay safe while we make sure he's safe, too. Do you remember you said you trusted me?"

"Yes. Because I thought you were on my side."

"I am on your side. And I need to keep both you and Hunter safe. I can't do my best for him if I'm worried about you, too."

"Then don't worry about me," she said. "The only person you need to worry about is Hunter."

He cupped her cheek in his palm. "I can't avoid worrying about you. That's how important you've become to me."

MISSING IN BLUE MESA

CINDI MYERS

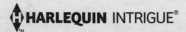

For Vicki

ISBN-13: 978-1-335-63899-1

Missing in Blue Mesa

Copyright © 2018 by Cynthia Myers

PLEASE RECYCLE
THIS PRODUCT IS RECYCLABLE

Recycling programs
for this product may
not exist in your area.

This edition published by arrangement with Harlequin Books S.A.

For questions and comments about the quality of this book, please contact us at CustomerService@Harlequin.com.

® and TM are trademarks of Harlequin Enterprises Limited or its corporate affiliates. Trademarks indicated with ® are registered in the United States Patent and Trademark Office, the Canadian Intellectual Property Office and in other countries.

Printed in U.S.A.

Cindi Myers is the author of more than fifty novels. When she's not crafting new romance plots, she enjoys skiing, gardening, cooking, crafting and daydreaming. A lover of small-town life, she lives with her husband and two spoiled dogs in the Colorado mountains.

Books by Cindi Myers

Harlequin Intrigue

The Ranger Brigade: Family Secrets

Murder in Black Canyon
Undercover Husband
Manhunt on Mystic Mesa
Soldier's Promise
Missing in Blue Mesa

The Men of Search Team Seven

Colorado Crime Scene
Lawman on the Hunt
Christmas Kidnapping
PhD Protector

The Ranger Brigade

The Guardian
Lawman Protection
Colorado Bodyguard
Black Canyon Conspiracy

Rocky Mountain Revenge
Rocky Mountain Rescue

Visit the Author Profile page at Harlequin.com.

CAST OF CHARACTERS

Ethan Reynolds—An FBI agent with special training in the behavior of cults, Ethan joined the Ranger Brigade in order to live closer to his widowed mom, but she's resisting his help.

Michelle Munson—Going by the name Starfall, she joined Daniel Metwater's group hoping to find clues about a murder. Growing up in the foster care system, she has learned to trust no one.

Hunter Munson—Michelle's infant son is the only person she has been able to love.

Daniel Metwater—The handsome, charismatic itinerant preacher left behind wealth and a life of ease in Chicago to lead his followers in the wilderness—but it appears he can carry a grudge too far.

David Metwater—Daniel's twin lived a life of debauchery and crime until he was murdered, supposedly by the Russian mafia.

Cass—Michelle's foster sister died of a drug overdose while with David Metwater, but Michelle is sure it was murder.

Tom and Thad Smith—They knew the Metwater brothers in Chicago. Was their move to Colorado a coincidence, or are they once again working for Daniel?

Andi Mattheson—The daughter of a senator, Andi left a life of privilege to take the name Asteria and follow Daniel Metwater, but recent happenings have begun to make her doubt the prophet.

Chapter One

She didn't have much time. No more than twenty minutes—probably less. No telling what would happen if he caught her in here. Everyone said he wasn't like his brother, but how could they be sure? The two were twins— identical twins. If one of them was a murderer, who was to say the other one wasn't capable of that, too?

Michelle jammed the piece of wire into the keyhole on the door to the motor home again and felt the catch give. She could thank Mom for that particular skill. How many times had she locked little Michelle out of their trailer while she was entertaining her boyfriend, or when she was sick of the kid? Then she'd get drunk and forget to let her back in.

Or that was what she said.

Better to thank Joey Staskavitch for teaching her how to pick the lock to get back in on her own. She wondered whatever happened to Joey. He was probably in jail, or dead. That was where most of the boys from her neighborhood had ended up.

Starfall—her real name was Michelle Munson, though nobody here knew that—pushed open the door to Daniel Metwater's motor home and stepped into the darkened living room. The noise from the festivities in the center of the encampment faded, though orange light from the bonfire cast grasping shadows across the walls and furniture. "Prophet" Daniel Metwater was dancing around the bonfire, leading his followers in mesmerizing chanting. They loved it. They could listen for hours to their Prophet's words about how they were special and better. Most of them had never been special to or better than anyone, but he made them believe it.

Michelle tiptoed across the room, headed for the back of the motor home, and Metwater's bedroom. That was where he would keep anything private. Anything he didn't want his adoring followers to know about.

The bedroom door, at least, wasn't locked. No one but his closest disciples were allowed in here—and the women he bedded, who considered it a privilege to sleep with the Prophet. Michelle wasn't one of those women. He had tried to seduce her when she first joined his little cult, but she'd put him off with a chilling stare. The gorgeous Daniel Metwater, like his twin, David, wasn't used to being turned down, but he must have seen something in her that made him wary, because after that he left her alone.

Alert for any sounds outside the room, she eased open the top dresser drawer and riffled through the contents. She worked quickly, passing over the clothing and toiletries. The bedside table held only books and sex toys. She wrinkled her nose. Not going to go there. She shut the drawer and hurried to the closet. Dropping to her knees, she felt along the floor and the back wall. That was where she would stick a safe, but all she encountered was two pairs of shoes and a pile of dirty clothes.

After glancing over her shoulder to make sure she was still alone, she flicked on the penlight she had tucked into the pocket of her jeans and swept the beam along the floor and up the walls. Nothing interesting there. Frowning, she rose. Where was the locket? Her tent mate, Asteria, Metwater's "secretary" and the person closest to him, had described it in such detail. "Gold, with a pear-shaped diamond in the center that is at least two carats," Asteria had said. She would know. Before hooking up with Metwater, she had been Andi Matheson, wealthy socialite and only daughter of a high-profile senator. She had seen her share of two-carat diamonds, though she claimed to now prefer the simple, nonmaterialistic life of following the Prophet through the wilderness. Right. Only people who had spent all their life around money could make a spiritual discipline out of giving it up.

"It looked old," Andi had said about the locket. "He said it was a family heirloom. He plans to give it to the baby after she's born." She had cradled her eight-months-pregnant belly and smiled. "To think that he loves her so much already that he'd want to give her something so valuable."

Michelle had to bite the inside of her cheek to keep from pointing out that Daniel Metwater didn't love anyone but himself. The locket was an heirloom, all right—but not from his family. Michelle's foster sister, Cass, had inherited the necklace from her grandmother. She had been wearing it the night she was murdered by David Metwater.

Michelle left the closet and returned to the

front room. She should have asked Asteria about a desk. Metwater probably had one, and maybe he kept the locket there. Maybe he had other things that had belonged to his brother, too—papers or a diary or anything Michelle might be able to use to prove that David had killed Cass.

The police said Cass had died of an accidental heroin overdose, but that wasn't true. She didn't do drugs. The night before she died, she had confided to Michelle that she had learned some things about her new boyfriend, David, that upset her. "I'm going to confront him," she said. "I need to know the truth."

The truth was, David Metwater had murdered Cass so that whatever she had learned about him wouldn't get out.

Michelle spotted the desk between the living and dining areas—a built-in shelf with a couple of drawers. A laptop sat open on the shelf, and her fingers itched to take it. She'd probably find all kinds of interesting information on that...

She shook her head. Too risky. She had come here for the locket, and time was running out. The drums outside had quieted, which meant the evening "services" were winding down. She pulled open the desk's center drawer and swept the beam of the penlight over the contents—paper clips, pencils, pens, business cards, a tube of lip balm—no locket. She shut the drawer and was reaching for another when light flooded the room. She froze, heart hammering painfully, unable to breathe.

"What do you think you're doing?" Daniel Metwater demanded.

Michelle turned to face him, but before she could reply, he crossed the room in four strides and grabbed her by the shoulders. His normally handsome face was a mask of rage. He shook her so hard she bit her tongue, tasting blood. *I'm dead*, she thought, as she stared into his cold, hard eyes. *I'll never see my son again.*

SPECIAL AGENT ETHAN REYNOLDS, FBI, stared down at the collection of half a dozen battered metal license plates arranged on the conference table at the headquarters of the Ranger Brigade, the multi-agency task force he was attached to. Before joining the Rangers, who were responsible for dealing with crime on the vast stretches of federal land in southwestern Colorado, Ethan had never realized how many criminals operated in the relatively deserted interior of national parks, wilderness preserves and protected recreation areas.

"You've verified these are all from stolen cars?" he asked his fellow agent, Immigration and Customs Enforcement Officer Simon Woolridge.

"Every one," Simon said. "A wildlife biologist with the Forest Service found them in an abandoned badger den near the end of Redvale Road. The Forest Service laid down a traffic counter on that road a couple of weeks ago and noticed heavier-than-expected traffic, so they were on the lookout for anything unusual."

"That's right about when this latest rash of thefts started," Ethan said. "So the thieves take the stolen cars to that remote area and strip the plates—then what?"

"Replace them with new tags," Simon said. "Probably forged dealer tags. They could print those up on any laser printer. Then they wait until dark and drive them out again, to a chop shop or even straight to Mexico."

"Then we need to stake out the site and grab them when they show up again," Ethan said.

"Unless they've moved on to a different location," Simon said. "The heavy rains two days ago washed out the road pretty badly. It doesn't look as if anyone has been up there since that storm. My guess is they're still in the area, but they've relocated."

Ethan glanced toward the large map of the Rangers' territory that filled one wall of the conference room. "How do we find that location?"

"We've alerted the park Rangers and the Forest Service, and anyone else who's likely to be in the area to be on the lookout for cars with dealer tags and anything meeting the description of the stolen vehicles," Simon said. He stabbed a finger at a point on the map. "The biologist found the license plates here. Does the location make you think of anything?"

"It's very near Daniel Metwater's camp at the base of Mystic Mesa." Ethan nodded to the red flag someone had positioned on the map. Metwater, scion of a wealthy industrialist and self-styled Prophet, had finagled a long-term camping permit for himself and roughly twenty followers in the Curecanti National Recreation area.

"It's less than ten miles by road," Simon said. "You could travel between the two sites over a network of old logging roads without ever having to risk being seen on the highway."

"That doesn't mean Metwater or any of his people had anything to do with the car thefts," Ethan said.

"No, but it doesn't mean they didn't," Simon

said. "I find it interesting how many recent crimes have a connection to that bunch."

"Metwater would point out that he's never been convicted of a crime," Ethan said. Not that he didn't agree with Simon. He had made a study of cults as part of his FBI training and he knew that groups like Metwater's attracted the disaffected and disenfranchised. Some people in the group would have less respect for laws and authority. A certain smaller percentage would be criminally dangerous.

"My mother thinks I never swear," Simon said. "That doesn't mean it's true."

"Do you plan on questioning Metwater?" Ethan asked.

"I thought we should drive over to his camp tonight and see if anyone is missing—someone who might be out boosting cars in the dark."

"I like the way you think," Ethan said. He hadn't been to the camp in a few weeks. The Rangers were under orders not to harass Metwater and his followers, though each side had different definitions of what constituted harassment. Metwater felt the presence of any member of the Ranger Brigade anywhere near his camp infringed on his rights to live as he pleased. The Rangers contended Metwater and his followers were potential witnesses to any of the many crimes that occurred on public lands, by virtue of being the only people living in the area.

They took Simon's FJ Cruiser, heading out of the national park and into the adjacent Curecanti National Recreation Area, toward the distinctive mesa where Metwater had made his camp. Forty minutes later Simon parked the cruiser between a rusting pickup and a doorless Jeep in the lot outside Metwater's camp. He switched off the headlights, and inky blackness closed around them. The moon hadn't yet risen, and though what looked like a million stars sparkled overhead, they didn't give much light. The two men waited a moment for their eyes to adjust to the darkness. Ethan breathed in deeply the scents of sagebrush and wood smoke. "Ready?" Simon asked.

"Ready."

They made their way up a narrow path toward the camp. Something skittered into the underbrush to Ethan's left and he flinched, hand on the butt of the Glock on his hip, then forced himself to relax when he realized it was only an animal—maybe a fox or a raccoon. Voices drifted to them as they neared the camp. They emerged into a clearing surrounded by more than a dozen trailers, tents and cobbled-together shacks. The remains of a bonfire glowed in a stone-lined pit in the center of the area, and the shadows of adults and children flitted about the dwellings, voices rising at the officers' approach.

Metwater lived in the large, modern motor home at one end of the camp. A pregnant young woman with long blond hair emerged from the white tent next to the motor home, a flashlight in one hand. Ethan recognized Andi Matheson, a former socialite and senator's daughter, who had taken the name Asteria when she moved in with Metwater.

"Miss Matheson."

She jerked her head up when Simon addressed her, and froze. "Is something wrong, Officers?" she asked.

"Just a routine patrol." Simon stopped in front of her, his lanky frame towering over her.

"At this time of night?" she asked, her expression angry.

"People think they can get away with things with the darkness to hide them," Simon said. "We like to catch them by surprise."

"You won't find anyone trying to get away

with anything here." She tried to move around him, but he took a step to the side, blocking her.

"So everyone is tucked tight in their beds?" Simon asked. "No one missing?"

"I don't keep track of everyone." She darted around him and walked past Ethan. The two men turned and followed her to the motor home. She stopped at the bottom of the steps and looked at them. "You can't see the Prophet without an appointment," she said.

"We know Mr. Metwater is always happy to cooperate with an investigation," Simon said. Did Asteria note the sarcasm in his voice?

"What investigation?" she asked.

"Have you seen any strange cars around camp?" Ethan asked. "Newer models? Anybody in the group get a new ride recently?"

"No. What is this about?"

"Maybe Metwater will know." Ethan had started to move past her when the door burst open and a woman stumbled out. She caught her foot on the top step and fell—right into Ethan's arms.

He staggered under the impact, but managed to stay upright and hold on to the woman. She stared up at him, eyes wide and full of terror, dark, curly hair a tangle around her sharp-featured face. Blood trickled from one corner of her mouth.

"Hey, it's okay." Ethan spoke softly. "What happened?"

The terror in her eyes didn't abate. "Help me," she whispered, before slipping into unconsciousness.

Chapter Two

Michelle fought past the fog that surrounded her, struggling back into consciousness. She had to flee or something terrible would happen. She opened her eyes and stared into the face of a man she didn't know. A new wave of fear revved her heart and she tried to pull away from him.

"Shh. It's okay." His voice was soft, his hands gentle, even as he continued to hold her arm. "Look at me," he said. "My name is Ethan. Ethan Reynolds. I'm not going to hurt you."

She stared into moss-green eyes so full of compassion and tenderness, tears burned at the back of her throat. She never cried. Crying was a sign of weakness and she couldn't afford to be weak. Especially not now.

She pushed herself into a sitting position on

the cot where she had been lying, though he kept one hand on her arm, steadying her. They were in the tent she shared with Asteria. Someone had lit the big oil lamp that hung from a post in the center of the room, a wavering circle of yellow light shining down on them. She had only a vague memory of rushing out of the motor home and falling... A fresh shudder of terror rocked her at the recollection.

"You must have hurt your head when you fell," Asteria said. She sat on the cot beside Michelle and pressed a wet washrag to the side of her face.

Michelle winced as pain radiated across her cheek and jaw. "I don't remember," she lied.

Out of the corner of her eye, she watched the man, Ethan. He had released his hold on her and moved to sit at the end of the cot. He had short, dark hair and good shoulders that filled out his khaki uniform shirt in a way she would have admired if she had been less distracted. As it was, he studied her with an intensity that sent a tremor through her. His eyes reflected compassion, but danger, too. "You didn't fall," he said. "Someone hit you. Was it Daniel Metwater?"

She closed her eyes, but she couldn't shut out the memory of Daniel Metwater's handsome face twisted in rage, his fists slamming into her over and over, pummeling her toward the door. He had demanded to know why she was in his trailer and she had foolishly blurted the truth. "I want the locket," she said. "Cass's locket. I know you have it."

After that she had been sure he would beat her to death. What if he came after her again? The thought made her stomach flip.

"The Prophet would never hurt anyone," Asteria protested. She stood, the damp cloth she had been holding to Michelle's face landing on the rug beside the cot with a soft *plop.* "He doesn't believe in violence."

"Tell anyone about this and you're dead." Metwater's parting words came back to Michelle. "You'll go out for a walk one day and no one will ever see you again. Mention that locket again and your son will die. You'll never see him again."

Part of her had been as naive as Asteria, believing Metwater would never hit her. She had been so wrong. "Hunter!" Suddenly frantic, she looked around for the child. "Where is Hunter?"

"He's right here." Michelle hadn't realized that a fourth person was in the room, another in the circle of women who had been drawn to

Metwater. Sarah stepped forward, the smiling little boy in her arms. He held out his chubby arms to Michelle and she gathered him close, burying her nose against his neck and inhaling that sweet baby smell.

"What's your name?" Ethan asked. "Your real name?"

They were supposed to only use their Family names with the cops. It was one of Metwater's rules. "You have a new identity now," he had preached. "The police don't need to know anything about your past." She was done with obeying his rules.

"It's Michelle," she said. "Michelle Munson."

Ethan stood and began pacing. He stopped in front of her, taller than she had thought before, radiating masculine power and suppressed anger—anger not at her but on her behalf. "Did Daniel Metwater hit you?" he asked again.

She closed her eyes and rested her cheek against Hunter's face. He was the only good thing that had ever happened to her and she would do anything to protect him. "I fell," she said.

Ethan pressed his lips together, clearly not

pleased with her answer. "If he hit you, I can arrest him and charge him with assault."

And he would be back in camp before lunchtime tomorrow. Daniel Metwater had plenty of money to pay a top lawyer. He would come back, and he would make sure Michelle paid for her betrayal. She raised her eyes to meet Ethan's, her gaze steady, giving away nothing. "The Prophet doesn't believe in violence," she said.

"What were you doing at the Prophet's place, anyway?" Asteria asked. "You were supposed to be at the fire circle with the rest of us."

Did Ethan hear the fear behind the question? Asteria worried she was losing her position as the Prophet's favorite.

"I went to him for counseling," Michelle said, though she knew the answer wouldn't ease Asteria's fears. Daniel Metwater sometimes "counseled" young women in his bed. He had never pretended to be faithful to Asteria, or to anyone else, but the poor girl apparently couldn't stop hoping.

Ethan sat beside Michelle on the cot once more. Hunter turned his head to look at the man, the little boy's eyes wide with curiosity. "How old is he?" Ethan asked. He offered his finger and, grinning, Hunter took hold of it.

His question caught her off guard. Was he really interested in her son, or only trying to lull her into trusting him? "Nine months," she answered.

"Taking care of a child by yourself is a big responsibility," Ethan said.

"I can handle it." She pulled Hunter closer.

"Looks like you're doing a great job." He freed his finger from the little boy's grasp, and his eyes met hers once more. "If you get hurt you won't be able to look after him."

She ignored the shudder that went up her spine at his words. She didn't need this cop warning her about how to behave. She had been looking after herself for a long time. She jutted out her chin. "I'll be fine."

"Be careful, that's all." He took a business card from his shirt pocket and held it out to her. "If you ever need help, or just want to talk, call me. Anytime."

She took the card and closed her fingers around it. People said things like that all the time, but they almost never meant it. But maybe Ethan Reynolds did.

He touched the cut on her lip, the lightest brush of his fingers, sending a shimmer of heat through her. "If you tell me who did this, I promise I won't let him hurt you again," he murmured.

"It was just clumsiness," she said. Clumsy of her not to guess how Metwater would react to her taunts about the locket. "It won't happen again." She wouldn't make the mistake of being alone with the Prophet again. He had lashed out so fiercely he had taken her by surprise, but next time she would be smarter. She would find a way to get the proof she needed that his brother had killed Cass. When she did, she would do everything in her power to make sure he never hit a woman again.

ETHAN EMERGED FROM the tent to find Simon waiting for him. "I was about ready to come in there after you," Simon said. He glanced over Ethan's shoulder. "What happened? How is Asteria and the other one—Stardust or whatever she calls herself?"

"Starfall. Michelle. Her real name is Michelle. She's pretty bruised up, and obviously terrified, though she's trying not to show it. Asteria is fine. Concerned for her friend, of course."

"What happened to her?" Simon asked. "To Starfall?"

"She says she fell, but I think somebody beat

her." He shifted his gaze to Metwater's motor home. No light shone from inside the dwelling.

"I didn't get anything out of any of the people who were still standing around here," Simon said. "They say they were at the bonfire and didn't see or hear anything."

"Let's see what Metwater has to say." Ethan started toward the motor home.

"I knocked, but no one answered," Simon said, falling in step beside Ethan. "I figured I'd wait for backup before I broke down the door."

"Maybe it won't come to that." Ethan pounded the door, a thunderous sound in the still darkness. "Open up!" he shouted. "Police!"

No answer.

Ethan glanced back at Simon, who had already drawn his weapon. "Metwater has a license for a handgun," Simon said. "I'd just as soon not give him a chance to use it."

Ethan nodded and drew his Glock. "On three," he said. "One. Two. Three." He hit the door hard, landing a fierce kick beside the lock, the metal crumpling under the blow. He hit it again with his shoulder and it burst inward. He immediately ducked around the jamb, waiting for an explosion of gunfire that didn't come.

Simon's eyes met his and he nodded. Ethan

went in first, gun at the ready, Simon at his back. Simon hit the light switch, illuminating a sofa, recliner, table and lamp. Nothing out of order and no obvious place for anyone to hide. Adrenaline making him hyperalert, Ethan pounded down the hallway to another door. He didn't bother knocking, but burst in, onto a scene of chaos.

A man cursed and a woman screamed— and kept on screaming. Ethan flicked the wall switch to the left of the door, and a single bedside lamp glowed, revealing a young woman standing in the corner, frantically trying to cover herself with a sheet she had dragged from the bed. Her mouth was open, and tears streamed down her face.

Daniel Metwater, naked and red-faced, sat up on the side of the bed. "Freeze!" Simon ordered, and fixed his weapon on him.

Metwater glared at them. "What is the meaning of this? The district attorney has ordered you people to leave me alone. I'll have your jobs, and then I'll sue you for everything you own. I—"

"Shut up," Ethan said. "And keep your hands where we can see them."

Metwater looked as if he might argue, but finally raised his hands to shoulder level. But he didn't stop talking. "You can't bust into a man's home in the middle of the night for no reason," he said.

"Shut up." Simon gave the order this time.

Ethan addressed the woman. "Are you all right, ma'am?" he asked.

She closed her mouth and swallowed, then nodded.

"What's your name?" Ethan asked.

"Sunshine."

"What's your full name?" he asked. "Your real name."

"Sunshine is my real name. Sunshine Hartford."

She looked barely eighteen, with strawberry-blond curls and freckles. "Ms. Hartford, how long have you been here with Mr. Metwater?" Ethan asked.

"N…not long." She pulled the sheet up higher over her breasts.

"How long?" Ethan asked. "Give me your best estimate."

"She's been here almost an hour," Metwater said.

"I told you to be quiet," Simon said.

"How long have you been here?" Ethan asked again.

"I guess like he said." She bit her bottom lip and glanced at Metwater. "About an hour?"

She was lying, but there wasn't much Ethan could do about it now. Confident Simon had Metwater under control, he holstered his Glock and took out a small notebook. "Give me your contact information and then you can get dressed and wait for us outside," he said.

He waited until the young woman had gathered her clothing and left the room, the sheet still wrapped around her. Then he turned to Metwater again. "Get up and put on some pants," he ordered.

With a sneering look, Metwater scooped a pair of loose-fitting white trousers from the floor and tugged them on. He tied the cord at the waist. "What are you doing here?" he asked.

"What happened between you and one of your followers—a woman called Starfall?" Ethan asked.

The expression in Metwater's icy brown eyes never changed. "What about her? If she's gotten into some kind of trouble, that's her problem, not mine."

"Not very sympathetic for a man who claims to be the head of a family," Simon said.

"We witnessed her coming out of this motor

home less than half an hour ago," Ethan said. "She was bruised and bleeding. She fainted."

"I don't know why she would be here." Metwater looked around, found a shirt and pulled it on, but didn't button it.

"I didn't ask if you knew why she was here," Ethan said. "What happened while she was here? How was she hurt?"

"I have no idea."

"Where were you when she was hurt?" Simon asked.

Metwater shrugged. "Since I don't know when she was hurt, or even if she was hurt, I can't answer that."

"Where were you thirty minutes ago?" Ethan asked.

"I already told you—I was here with Miss Hartford."

"So you admit you were here, in this motor home, at the time Starfall was hurt," Ethan said. "Yet you don't know how she was hurt?"

Metwater's smile held no warmth. "I was otherwise occupied. With Miss Hartford."

"Is Miss Hartford one of your followers?" Simon asked. "I don't remember seeing her around before."

"She's an aspiring disciple," Metwater said.

"We're going to question Ms. Hartford," Ethan said. "Are you sure she'll confirm your story?"

"She will."

Ethan fought the urge to knock the smug look off Metwater's face. "Did you have an argument with Starfall?" he asked.

"No." His smile faded. "Does she say that we did?"

"She's too upset to question right now," Ethan said. He wanted to keep Metwater off guard as much as possible.

"She'll confirm we didn't argue," Metwater said. "Unless she lies. She sometimes has a problem with honesty. It's something we're working on."

"I'll find out the truth," Ethan said. "And I'll make sure the person who hurt Starfall is charged and prosecuted."

"Knock yourself out, Officer." Metwater stood. "But now it's time for you to leave. Expect to hear from my lawyers."

Ethan took a step toward Metwater. If this so-called Prophet thought Ethan was going to be intimidated by empty threats, he was in for a rude awakening.

"Come on." Simon's voice snapped Ethan out of his rage. "We're wasting our time here."

Ethan turned and led the way out of the

motor home. "I wanted to deck him, too," Simon said when they were outside. "But it wouldn't be worth the hassle the suits would put you through later."

Ethan nodded and took a deep, calming breath. "We should talk to Ms. Hartford," he said.

"She's long gone." Simon looked around at the empty campground. The only light was from the few dying embers of the bonfire, and a thin glow of gold showing at the entrance to Asteria and Starfall's tent. "We'll track her down tomorrow."

"I want to check on Starfall one more time," Ethan said.

Asteria met them at the door of the tent. "She's sleeping," she said, in answer to Ethan's unvoiced question. "She was pretty shaken up, but I think she'll be okay. She's pretty tough."

"Did she tell you anything about what happened?" Ethan asked.

Asteria tucked her hair behind one ear. Deep shadows hollowed her eyes and she looked exhausted. "She wouldn't say anything. She got angry when I asked her about it."

"Has Daniel Metwater ever hit any of the women in camp before?" Ethan asked.

Asteria gaped at them, wide-eyed. "No!

He would never do that! It isn't possible." She smoothed back her hair. "I should go to him now. He'll be very upset about your accusations, and he's expecting me. I was on my way to him when all this happened." She waved a hand toward the cot where Starfall slept.

She started to move past them, but Simon put out a hand to stop her. "What do you mean, Metwater is expecting you?" he asked.

Defiance shone behind the fatigue. "I was going to spend the night with him. I often do."

"If he was expecting you, what was Sunshine Hartford doing there?" Simon asked.

"Sunshine? Do you mean that girl who's been hanging around here?" Asteria furrowed her brow. "I thought I saw her at the fire circle tonight, but she wasn't with the Prophet."

"She was with him a few minutes ago," Ethan said.

"She was with him in his bed," Simon added.

Asteria stared at him. "What?"

"He told us he and Ms. Hartford had been together for the last hour," Simon said.

"That can't be right," she said.

"Why can't it be right?" Ethan asked.

"Because..." She bit her lower lip, then shook her head. "Just, because." She looked back toward the cot. Starfall lay on her side, the blanket pulled up past her ears. Only the tumble of her brown curls showed against the white of the pillow.

Simon touched Asteria's elbow, turning her attention back to him. "Why can't it be right?" he asked.

"He was supposed to be alone!" The words burst from her, and her eyes shone wetly. "Not with Starfall or Sunshine or anyone else. He asked me to come to him."

"Maybe he had something else in mind for tonight," Simon said.

She shook her head. "No. He isn't like that. You don't know him at all or you wouldn't say something like that."

"Maybe you don't know him that well, either," Simon said.

She stepped back into the tent. "Go away and leave us alone," she said. "You're not welcome here."

"We'll leave for now," Simon said. "But think about what's happened tonight. If Daniel Metwater would lie to you about being alone tonight, what else has he lied to you about?"

Ethan gave her a hard look. "And what are you going to do to stop the lying?"

Chapter Three

Michelle was still on Ethan's mind the next morning as he made his way down the quiet residential street on Montrose's south side. Staying emotionally distant from victims was a necessary part of the job—let yourself get too wound up about the things people did to each other and you'd never sleep at night. But Michelle got to him. She looked so wounded and fragile, yet he sensed real strength in her.

He turned onto his parents' street and nodded to a jogger on the sidewalk. The neighbor's sprinkler sent a shimmer of water over the perfectly trimmed yard, and the aroma of wet grass and pavement drifted in through his partially open window. He pulled into the driveway, wondering how long it would be before he stopped expecting to see his father waiting at the front door. Dad had been gone six months now, but every time Ethan came to the house he experienced that jolt of expectation followed by disappointment.

His mother came to the front door and held open the screen, waiting for him. She wore pale blue scrubs and white clogs, ready for her nursing shift at Montrose Hospital. She looked so small to him—smaller than she had been when he was a boy, and smaller than when his dad had been alive. She smiled as he approached and stood on tiptoe to kiss his cheek. "This is a nice surprise," she said. "What brings you out so early?"

"I just stopped by to see how you're doing."

"I'm fine. I went shopping yesterday and they had some nice melon. Would you like some?"

"That's okay, Mom. I already had breakfast." He looked back at the neighbor's sprinkler. "I'll try to come over this afternoon and mow the lawn," he said.

"You don't have to do that," she said. "I can hire someone. Mrs. Douglas across the street has someone. I can ask her who she uses."

"You don't have to do that, Mom. I'll take care of it." His dad had kept the place immaculate when he was alive—grass cut every week, hedges trimmed, flowers mulched. Dad paid all the bills and took care of the cars and even drove Mom shopping once a week. Now she was having to do all those things herself. Ethan wondered if it was too much for her.

"First chance I get, I'll change the oil in your car," he said as he followed her into the house. "It's probably past time for that."

"I can take it to one of those quick oil change places," she said. "You have enough to do without worrying about me."

But Ethan did worry. One of the reasons he had jumped at the chance to join the Ranger Brigade was that the new position would allow him to live close to his mom—to look after her.

"Do you have time for coffee?" she asked as she led the way to the kitchen. "I was just going to pour myself a cup."

"Coffee would be nice." He sat at the kitchen table—his usual spot, to the left of the chair where his father had always sat. From this position, he had a good view of the backyard, and the patio he and his dad had put in during Ethan's senior year of high school—a patio currently occupied by a trio of tabby cats, busy devouring a dish of crumpets.

"Still feeding the neighborhood strays, I see," he said.

"They're not strays." His mother slid a blue

mug of coffee in front of him, then took her seat in her usual place across from Ethan. "They're feral cats. They've never had a home, but grew up in the wild."

One cat finished and retreated to a fence post to groom itself in the sun. "You planning on adopting them?" Ethan asked. A pet might be good for her, keep her company.

"That's not how it works with ferals," she said. "You can't really tame them. They'll never give up their independence. The best I can do is feed them and provide a sheltered spot for them to get out of the weather." She indicated a pile of blankets in a corner of the covered patio.

"Sounds like a good way to end up with a whole zoo of wild cats," Ethan said.

"Oh, no. They've all been neutered. See how their ears are notched? That tells everyone they were fixed."

The cat on the post did indeed have a notch cut out of its right ear. "Maybe you should think about adopting a domestic cat, then," he said. "Wouldn't you enjoy the company?"

"I enjoy feeding the ferals and having them around, without the commitment to a full-time cat," she said.

"Just be careful, Mom," he said. "Don't let one of them bite you or anything."

"You sound just like your father."

Though she was smiling, the remark pained him. The reaction must have shown on his face, because she quickly changed the subject. "How is your new job going?" she asked. "Are you working on anything interesting?"

"We're trying to track down some car thieves we think might be operating on public land." He sipped the coffee. "We were out at Daniel Metwater's camp last night, seeing if they knew anything."

"He's that good-looking preacher fellow, isn't he?" His mom shook a packet of sweetener into her coffee and stirred. "I've read things about him in the paper—all those young people camping out with him. Just like the hippies back when I was that age." She laughed. "One summer your father decided to grow his hair long and your grandmother was worried to death that he was going to become one of those flower children."

"Dad had long hair?" Ethan couldn't picture it. For most of his life, his dad hadn't had much hair at all.

"Oh, it was just one summer," she said. "Then he got a job in the oil fields and he had to cut it. I quite liked it, though. He had prettier hair than I did." She laughed again. "What are they like, the followers of that Prophet?"

"Mostly young," he said. "Some men, but a lot of women and children. Most of them are probably harmless, but he's attracted his share of people who are running from something—including the law."

"I can't think the children have much of a life, camping in the woods like that," she said.

"We try to monitor them, make sure there's no abuse or neglect." He frowned, remembering the bruises on Michelle's face.

"What is it, dear?" his mother asked. "You look upset."

"Last night when we were out there, we ran into a woman," he said. "Or rather, she ran into us. She'd been beaten—pretty badly. But she insisted she had fallen and wouldn't tell us who had hit her."

"Oh, no." His mom made a tsking noise. "We get women like that in the emergency room sometimes. They're too afraid to tell the truth, I think."

"This woman was afraid." He pushed his half-empty cup aside. "I'm going to go out there this morning and talk to her again. Maybe I can persuade her to file charges."

"I hope you can help her," his mom said. "No woman should be treated that way. Your father would have died before he raised his hand against me."

"Yeah, Dad was a great guy." He pushed his chair back. "I'd better get going. I'll be over later to take care of the lawn."

His mom walked with him to the door. "Thanks, sweetie." She kissed his cheek again. "And don't worry about me. That's my job."

It was his job, too, now that his dad wasn't around. Trying to ignore the heaviness in his chest, he returned to his cruiser. He couldn't take away his mom's or his own grief, but he could do whatever he could to make her life easier. She wasn't like Michelle—alone with no one to defend her.

MICHELLE WOKE TO Hunter's crying—a reassuring sound, since she had been having a dream in which he was lost and she couldn't find him. She sat up on the side of her cot, groaning as pain radiated through her body, and the memory of last night returned, like a fresh blow. She put a hand to the tender, swollen flesh around her mouth, and carefully stood, then shuffled toward the crib.

The baby was soaking wet, so she changed

him, then sat on the side of the cot once more to nurse him. She was weaning him, but right now she needed this closeness, giving him something only she could provide. Asteria was nowhere in sight—not surprising, since she spent most of her nights lately with Daniel Metwater. Michelle held her son closely and replayed the events of last night in her head.

She had been stupid to think Metwater wouldn't lash out at her. Stupid to believe he would hand over the locket in exchange for her promise of silence. Not that she intended to keep that promise, but she was good at conning people. She had been doing it most of her life.

But Metwater was a con, too. He knew how the game was played. And now that he knew she was on to him, she would have to be careful. She would have to make sure Hunter stayed safe.

She brushed the hair from the baby's forehead and he smiled up at her. Her heart clenched. Until she had had Hunter, she had had nothing—no one.

She slipped a hand into her pocket and felt the business card the Ranger had given her. Ethan. A high-class-sounding name. Someone named Ethan probably wouldn't drop out of school or end up in jail for boosting cars or dealing drugs, the way the boys from her neighborhood did. Ethan went to college. He got a job upholding the law instead of breaking it.

Ethan didn't look twice at Michelle Munson from the wrong side of town. But Ethan Reynolds had looked at her. She had stared into his eyes and felt that he was seeing her—not the cool, smart-talking tough girl role she had assumed before her age reached double digits, but the real her—the woman who had been hurt, who was fearful of a future she couldn't control. Most of the time she forgot that woman even existed anymore, but somehow this cop had seen it.

The knowledge made her feel vulnerable—a sensation she didn't like. She was the only person she could rely on to look after herself and her son. That meant she couldn't let anyone make her feel helpless. Daniel Metwater controlled people by making them believe they weren't capable of making the right choices for their lives. They needed him to make those choices for them—to control their money and tell them when to eat and what to think. When she had first come here, she was amazed at how many people were willing to give up everything to someone who promised to make them feel good.

The flap of the tent pushed open and Asteria ducked inside. She carried a cup of coffee and handed it to Michelle. "I thought you might need this," she said.

"Yes. You're a saint." Michelle took the cup and drained a third of it in one long swallow. At least the Prophet hadn't made them give up coffee, the way he had talked them into giving up meat two days a week and cell phones and movies, and she had lost track of how much else. If she hadn't promised herself she would do whatever she had to in order to prove that Cass was murdered, she would have left this place a long time ago.

"How are you feeling?" Asteria sat on the cot beside her.

"A little sore." She watched Asteria out of the corner of her eye as she spoke. She had to be careful here. She couldn't afford to upset Metwater's biggest fan. "That was some fall."

"What were you doing at the Prophet's trailer?" Asteria asked. "And don't give me that lie about counseling."

"Why don't you believe I went to him for counseling?" Michelle asked.

"Because you're not the counseling type. You don't confide in people."

No, she didn't. And even if she did, she wouldn't reveal anything personal to a man like Metwater. She didn't want him to know so much as her shoe size, in case he could find a way to use it against her. "I went there to complain," she said. "The men in this camp are lazy bums who don't do their share of the work. He needs to put some of them on kitchen duty, instead of making us look after the children and prepare all the meals while they sit around and wait to be fed." She had no trouble getting into this rant, since it was one she had voiced before. The other women agreed with her, but none of them were willing to do anything about it.

Most of the tension went out of Asteria's shoulders. "You shouldn't bother him with something like that," she said. "Not late at night."

"It wasn't that late." She shifted Hunter to her other arm and took another drink of coffee. "Anyway, he wasn't there."

"If he wasn't there, why did you go inside?"

"The door was unlocked. I only stepped into the living room and called for him. I mean, it wasn't like I was going to go into his bedroom or anything." She held her breath, hoping Asteria would believe her.

"So you didn't see him at all?"

"No. I waited a few seconds, then turned and left. I must have caught my foot on the step on my way out." The cop, Ethan, hadn't believed that lame story for even a minute, but Asteria was buying it the way the former socialite would once have snagged a coveted designer gown in her size.

"Did you see anyone else?" Asteria asked. "Either in the motor home or on your way there?"

Someone else? That was an interesting development. "Who?" she asked.

"Did you see Sunshine?"

"Sunshine?" Starfall tried and failed to match a face to that name.

"The girl who's been hanging around lately."

Ah! The girl who had been shamelessly flirting with Metwater. Starfall saw where this was going now. "No, I didn't see her," she said. She hadn't seen anyone but Metwater and his fist.

"I knew those Rangers were lying," Asteria said. "They told me that when they questioned the Prophet about what had happened to you, he told them he was with Sunshine. They were just trying to upset me so that I would tell lies about the Prophet."

If you're sleeping with a guy, it's probably okay to call him by his first name, Michelle thought, but she kept quiet. Asteria—the former Andi Matheson—had bought Metwater's line about being a holy seer one hundred percent. She was his favorite follower—and also his wealthiest—and she couldn't even see the connection between his favoritism and her money. "What kind of lies did they want you to tell?" she asked.

"That he hit you. Which is ridiculous, because you know how much he hates violence."

Right. "I've heard him say several times that he hates violence," she agreed. Though he had had no trouble trying to beat her brains in last night. She still wasn't sure how she had managed to break free and run for the door. If the two Rangers hadn't been standing right outside, would he have pursued her and maybe even killed her?

She set down her coffee mug, suddenly sick to her stomach. "I need to take a shower," she said. Some of the men had built a shower shack at the other end of camp. Water came from a plastic barrel that sat on top of the shack. The sun heated the water, and the plastic showerhead had an on-off switch that allowed the person showering to control the flow. It wasn't the Ritz, but it wasn't bad.

"Do you want me to watch Hunter while you do that?" Asteria asked.

"That's okay. I'll take him in with me." Hunter liked to sit on the floor and play in the puddles that collected around her feet. Until she was sure she was safe, she wasn't going to let the baby out of her sight.

She finished the coffee, then collected a towel, soap and shampoo, and picked up Hunter. "Let's go take a shower, buddy," she said, bouncing him on her hip. He giggled, dimples forming on either side of his mouth. Smiling in return, she headed toward the shower shack.

She had just turned onto the path to the shower when Daniel Metwater stepped out in front of her. She stumbled to a halt, heart racing, searching for a way out. But the woods grew close to the path on either side and Metwater blocked the way forward. She could turn and run, but he might be able to catch her.

She stood, frozen, as he approached and put a hand on her shoulder. "I heard you had a bad fall," he said, gaze focused on her bruises. "Are you all right?"

The absurdity of his words, and the false concern in his voice, shocked her out of her fear. She stumbled back, wrenching away from him. "No, I am not all right." She checked to make sure no one was close enough to overhear them. "And I didn't fall. You and I both know it."

"As long as no one else knows." He wrapped his hand around Hunter's arm. Now if she tried to pull away, the baby would be hurt. "I meant what I told you," he said. "If you want Hunter to stay safe, you won't say a word about this—or about that locket—to anyone."

She wanted to spit in his face—to tell him that she was going to expose his brother as a murderer and him as a fraud. But she couldn't do that. She had to protect her son, and find a way to keep them both safe until she could get the proof she needed. "I know how to keep my mouth shut," she said. "I haven't told anyone about what I know, and I've been here for months."

"Make sure you don't."

She left, wanting to run but forcing herself to walk. She could feel his gaze boring into her back all the way to the shower shack, and when she reached the shack and glanced back, he was still watching, the hatred in his expression making her tremble all the way to her toes.

SUNSHINE HARTFORD VIBRATED like a terrified rabbit. Her left leg bounced and her upper lip twitched as she stared, wide-eyed, at the trio of officers gathered around her at Ranger Brigade Headquarters. Ethan and Agent Carmen Redhorse had picked her up at her apartment in Montrose and brought her in for questioning, thinking if they could rattle her a little she would be more likely to confess the truth.

But Ethan hadn't intended to frighten her so badly she couldn't speak. "You don't have anything to worry about, Miss Hartford," he tried to reassure her. "You haven't done anything wrong. We only want your help in drawing a clear picture of what happened last night at Daniel Metwater's motor home."

"A woman was injured." Carmen leaned toward the young woman, her voice soft but firm. "You can help us find who hurt her."

"I… I was with the Prophet," she stammered. "You saw me there."

"How long had you been with him?" Ethan asked.

"He told you. We had been there an hour."

"Yes, that's what he told us, but that can't

be right, can it?" Ethan tried to keep his tone conversational, nonaccusatory. "Was the bonfire even over that long?"

She squirmed like a kid who had to go to the bathroom. "I didn't have a watch with me."

"Did you hear or see anyone else in the motor home while you were there?" Ethan asked. "Maybe someone in another room?"

She shook her head. "No. When you're with the Prophet, it's as if no one else is around."

Out of view of Sunshine, Carmen rolled her eyes. "Did he say anything to you about anyone else?" Ethan asked. "Did he mention anyone by name?"

"He said if I saw Asteria, I had to pretend I hadn't been with him," she said.

"And you were okay with that?" Carmen asked. "Lying to another woman?"

"It wouldn't be lying, exactly," Sunshine said. "And I would be obeying the Prophet. You can't be a good disciple if you aren't obedient."

A classic manipulator's line, Ethan thought.

"Did you know that lying to the police is against the law?" Ethan asked.

"The Prophet answers to the highest law. I'm sure he wouldn't ask me to do anything harmful."

"So you admit you're lying," Ethan said.

Her expression clouded. "I haven't seen or spoken to Asteria," she said. "So I haven't had to lie about anything."

"What about how much time you spent with Metwater?" Carmen asked. "Are you lying about that?"

She wrinkled her nose, and her voice took on a strident edge. "I told you—I don't wear a watch. I wasn't keeping track of the time. He said it was an hour, so it must be an hour."

"All right," Ethan said. "Take me through the sequence of events last night. When did you arrive at camp?"

"The fire circle is always at dusk, so I got to the camp a little before—about eight thirty."

"What next?"

"I walked into camp. The bonfire was going and a lot of Family members were already there. I found some women I knew and stood with them. We waited about fifteen minutes and then the Prophet came out." A smile transformed her from sulky teen to beautiful woman. "He was wearing a loincloth and had painted his face. He was beautiful."

"And he does what at these fire circles?" Every cult had its rituals. The researcher in Ethan was curious about Metwater's rituals.

"First, he gave us a message about how we

should live. He talked about sharing—about how the rest of the world lives in an economy based on hoarding, but in the Family, everyone shares, and that makes everyone better off, instead of only a few people."

Carmen made a snorting noise. Sunshine gave her a sharp look. "Go on," Carmen said. "I didn't mean to interrupt."

"After the message, the drummers started up, and the Prophet led us in a chant. Then he began to dance. It was mesmerizing."

"What do the rest of you do while he dances?" Ethan asked.

"We chant. And sometimes the Prophet asks other people to dance with him." Her cheeks glowed pink. "Last night he asked me to dance with him. I was so excited I couldn't even feel my feet touch the ground."

"How long did you dance?" Ethan asked.

"Not long. We went around the fire and when we reached my place in the circle, the Prophet kissed my cheek. Everyone was watching and I felt so special." Her eyes shone with the memory. Metwater certainly had her under his spell.

"What happened next?" Ethan prompted.

"The chanting and dancing went on for a little while longer. Then the drums quieted and the Prophet gave us his blessing. Then everyone left the fire circle and went to bed."

"Where did you go?" Carmen asked. "Did you go with the Prophet?"

"Not right away. I stood around talking with some of the other women—Sarah and Moonglow—and a guy named Alex."

"What did you talk about?" Ethan asked.

"Nothing in particular. I wanted to know more about what it was like to live in the Family. I want to join, but the Prophet says they aren't taking any new members right now. Apparently, they had trouble with some cops pretending to be interested in joining and using that to spy on the group. Can you believe that?"

Ethan's eyes met Carmen's and he suppressed a smile. She had lived with Metwater and his followers for a couple of weeks last month, by pretending to be a prospective member. Her undercover work hadn't revealed any evidence of criminal activity in the group, but it had led to contact with a Fish and Game officer tracking smugglers. Carmen had helped with the case and now she and the Fish and Game cop were engaged.

"So you didn't go to Metwater's motor home with him right away?" he asked Sunshine.

"No. I stood around and talked for a while. I

was thinking I should probably go back to my car when the Prophet walked over and asked me to come back to his motor home with him." She blushed again. "Just like that, he singled me out. It was amazing."

"Did you see anyone or talk to anyone on your way to the motor home?" Ethan asked.

"No. He took my hand and practically dragged me back there with him."

"What happened when you got inside the motor home?" Ethan asked. "What did you see?"

"Nothing, really. He had all the lights turned off. He took me to his bedroom and told me to undress. He started undressing, too. We got under the covers and started making out. And then you interrupted."

"That doesn't sound like it would take an hour to me," Ethan said.

"I don't see why the time matters so much," Sunshine said. "The important thing is that we were together and I didn't see anybody else— certainly not a hurt woman. I mean, I'm sorry she was hurt, but the Prophet wouldn't do anything like that. He loves women."

"He certainly loves to use them," Carmen said.

Sunshine stood and brushed off her skirt. "Can I go now?" she asked.

"Yes, you can go," Ethan said. "I'll take you back home." He dug in his pocket for his car keys but stopped when the front door of Ranger Headquarters burst open.

Starfall staggered inside, her face pale as death except for the bruising along her jaw and around her mouth. She stared at Ethan with haunted eyes, and when she spoke, her voice was a ragged gasp. "Hunter…my baby…he's gone! You have to help me get him back!"

Chapter Four

Panic clawed at Michelle's throat and clouded her vision. Every breath burned and her pulse pounded in her head. *My baby's gone. My baby's gone. My baby's gone!*

A steadying hand gripped her arm and a man's firm but gentle voice cut through the clamor of her thoughts. "Take a deep breath. I'm going to help you. Sit down over here and tell me everything that happened."

Ethan Reynolds led her to a chair and someone brought her a cup of water. She drank it and struggled to control her breathing. "My little boy, Hunter, is missing," she said. "Daniel Metwater took him, I know he did. He threatened to hurt him and now he's done it." She choked back a sob.

Ethan sat in a chair across from her, his

knees almost touching hers, his hand firm on her shoulder. "Michelle, look at me," he said.

She looked into brown eyes so full of concern and compassion that a fresh flood of tears filled her eyes. "I know it's hard, but you have to be strong," he said. "The more information you can tell us, the more we'll have to use to find your baby. And we will do everything in our power to find him."

He was right. She had to be strong. And she was strong. She wouldn't have made it this long if she wasn't. She took a deep breath and began. "I was in the shower," she said. "We have this shower shack, with a plastic barrel of water on the roof. The sun warms the water and there's a showerhead with a switch you can turn on and off. I took Hunter into the stall with me. He likes to play in the water and I wanted to keep an eye on him." She had only turned away for a second...

"What happened then?" Ethan prompted, once more pulling her back from that awful abyss of panic.

"I had just turned on the water and was wetting my hair when someone dumped a bucket of paint over the side of the stall. The top is mostly open and I know there was some paint sitting around—the plan was to paint the shack, but no one had gotten around to it yet." She was rambling, filling in too many details, but she couldn't stop herself.

"Who dumped the paint—do you know?" A woman's voice this time. Michelle turned her head and recognized Carmen Redhorse—the cop who had lived with them for a while. She and Michelle hadn't exactly gotten along—Michelle had tried to scam the cop Carmen was now engaged to.

"I don't know who threw the paint," she said. "I couldn't see anything. That was the problem. I had paint all over me—in my hair and in my eyes. I screamed and I was trying to wash it all out. I was worried about it drying that way, in my hair and my eyelashes. I turned the water on full blast and grabbed the shampoo. I couldn't see or hear anything. By the time I got it all rinsed out, Hunter was gone. Someone must have reached in and grabbed him while I was blinded. Either Metwater or someone he ordered to take Hunter."

"Why do you think it was Metwater?" Ethan asked.

"Because he said he would hurt Hunter if I didn't keep quiet about what happened last night, and about what I knew about his brother."

"So he is the one who hurt you last night?" Ethan asked.

"Yes. But I couldn't tell you about it. I couldn't tell anyone. I kept quiet, the way he said." But it hadn't made any difference, apparently.

"What was that about his brother?" Ethan asked.

She sighed. How could she make this cop understand, when the story was so convoluted? But she had to try. "My sister, my foster sister, Cass, dated Daniel Metwater's twin brother, David. She thought she was in love with him, but she was worried. She had found out something about him—something bad. She wouldn't tell me what it was, but she told me she was going to confront him. She thought this bad thing couldn't possibly be true, that he would prove it wasn't true and they could go on. Instead, she died that night of an apparent heroin overdose. But Cass didn't use drugs. I know she didn't. He killed her so she wouldn't reveal the bad thing she had found out about him. I'm sure of it."

"That's terrible," Carmen said. "But what does it have to do with Daniel Metwater?"

"Cass had a locket—gold, with a big diamond. She inherited it from her grandmother.

She was wearing it the night she disappeared, but when police found her body, the locket was missing. A few days ago Asteria told me Daniel had showed her a gold locket and promised to give it to her baby. It sounded like Cass's locket. If I could get hold of that, it would help me prove that there was a connection between Cass and the Metwaters. It might be enough to get the police to dig deeper into her death. More than anything, I want to clear her name and prove David Metwater was a murderer. It's why I joined up with the Family in the first place."

"So you went to Metwater's motor home last night to get the locket," Ethan said.

"Yes. Only he came back earlier than I expected and he caught me looking for it. He was furious. He started hitting me and telling me he was going to hurt Hunter, too. I thought he was going to beat me to death. Somehow I broke free and ran out of the trailer—that's when you found me."

"Why didn't you tell me any of this last night?" Ethan asked. She heard the frustration in his voice—she couldn't blame him.

"I was afraid of him," she said. "The way he beat on me, I'm sure he was ready to kill me. And I had to protect Hunter."

"Did Daniel Metwater specifically threaten to take Hunter?" Carmen asked.

"He said he would hurt him. He said it last night, and again this morning. He stopped me on the way to the showers and he said if I wanted Hunter to stay safe, I needed to keep my mouth shut. I told him I would, but I guess he didn't believe me."

"What did you do when you discovered Hunter was missing?" Ethan asked.

"I pulled on my clothes and ran out of the shower, calling for him. I thought maybe he wandered off. I stopped everyone I met and asked if they had seen him, but no one had. Then I went to Metwater's motor home and pounded on the door. I screamed that I wanted my baby. He said he didn't know anything about my baby and I needed to stop being so hysterical." She could have killed Metwater in that moment. She had tried to push past him, to search for Hunter, but he had two of his bodyguards hold her back. "I accused him of taking Hunter and he told everyone I had lost my mind. After that no one would help me, so I came here." She slumped forward, head in her hands. "I didn't know what else to do."

"We'll help you." Ethan took one hand and gently pulled it away from her face. "We'll put out an Amber Alert for Hunter. Everyone will be looking for him. We'll search the camp and we'll question Metwater. We'll find your son."

She nodded. If they acted quickly, maybe Metwater wouldn't have had time to take Hunter away somewhere.

"All those articles you had collected about David and Daniel Metwater," Carmen said. "The ones I found in your trunk—they were because of your sister?"

Michelle stared at the other woman for a moment, before she remembered that Carmen had, indeed, searched her trunk—and she had discovered the item Michelle had been using to blackmail the Fish and Game officer Carmen was now engaged to. "I didn't know you had seen the articles," she said.

"I didn't read them all," Carmen said. "But I looked through them enough to see they were all about Daniel and David Metwater. I thought maybe you were trying to blackmail him, too."

"I wish," Michelle said. "I saved every article I could find, hoping it would give me some clue as to what really happened to Cass that night. The local police wouldn't believe she had been murdered, so they weren't doing anything about it. It was up to me."

"So you decided to join Daniel Metwater's family," Ethan said.

"Yes. I called myself Starfall because I didn't want to risk Metwater recognizing the name. Cass and I weren't related by blood— her family took me in as their foster child when I was a teenager, but Cass might have mentioned me, so I thought it was safer to assume a fake name. A lot of the people who join his family do that. Asteria did it. She used to be some wealthy socialite."

"Do you mind if I call you Michelle?" Ethan asked. "At least when Metwater isn't around?"

She nodded. "I'd like that. Since he took my baby, I don't want to have anything to do with him." She sat up straighter. "And I don't care if he knows who I really am now. I'm not going to let him get away with this."

"Neither are we." Ethan's expression was grim. "I promise you—neither are we."

HALF AN HOUR later Ethan glanced over at the woman who sat in the passenger seat of his FJ Cruiser. Starfall—Michelle—was still pale, the bruises around her mouth from where Metwater had hit her last night a painful-looking purple. "You hanging in there?" he asked.

She nodded and turned toward him. "What do you think he's done with Hunter?"

"I don't know." It wasn't the answer she wanted, but it was all he had to give her. "Would Hunter have gone with him willingly, do you think?"

"Probably. He's a friendly boy, and he's never had any reason to be afraid of anyone or anything. I made sure of that."

"What about his father?"

She stiffened. "What about him?"

"Is it possible he would take the boy? That happens sometimes with custody disputes."

"No." She shook her head, curls bouncing. "He's been out of the picture for months now. He was a mistake."

"Still, he might decide he wants his son." Ethan couldn't imagine having a child who wasn't a part of his life. "What's his name? We can check his whereabouts."

"It's Greg Warbush. The last I heard he was in Seattle. But you're wasting your time looking for him. He wouldn't take Hunter. Greg was never even interested in him. He even said he wasn't sure Hunter was his." She shrugged. "Maybe he was right."

Ethan tried not to let his feelings show on his face, but his expression must have betrayed something, because she said, "I was in a bad place after Cass died. She was the only family I really had—the only person I was close to. I went off the deep end, drinking and sleeping around. I snapped out of it when I found out I was pregnant. I didn't want my kid growing up the way I had—unwanted. I straightened up and tried to make it work with Greg, but I guess when you start out that way, the relationship is doomed."

The way she said that word—*unwanted*—as if it was just another fact in her life—sent a chill through him. Ethan's parents had always been there for him. He couldn't imagine living a life where the only person you cared about—the only person you thought cared about you—was a foster sibling.

"Is there anyone else who might want to harm you or your son?" he asked. "Someone with a grudge against you? Someone who is angry with you, for whatever reason?"

She sighed and tilted her head back to stare up at the ceiling. "I'm sure you've talked to Officer Redhorse. If you have, you know I'm not the most popular person in camp. I'm not the kind of person who gets close to other people, and I've done things to make enemies."

"What kind of things?"

"I find out people's secrets and use that to get them to do what I want." Her eyes flashed, defiant.

"You mean blackmail?"

"Nobody in camp has any money. And most people don't have big secrets, either. But if I need a guy to fix my car and he says no, I'll snoop around until I catch him doing something like siphoning gas out of the Prophet's ride and I'll threaten to tell unless he make the repairs I need. I'm not saying I'm proud of it, but I do what I have to do to survive."

Part of him could admire her resourcefulness, even if he didn't approve of her methods. "By your silence, I can tell you don't approve," she said. "But don't worry. I promise I won't try to scam you."

"I think I'm smart enough to spot a scam," he said.

"Did I mention that I'm very, very good?"

Her teasing tone gave him hope—she was holding it together under horrendous circumstances. That told him more about her strength than any show of force. "Thanks for warning me," he said.

ONLY A COUPLE of vehicles sat in the parking area outside Metwater's camp. Ethan parked his vehicle, and two other Ranger units slid in beside him. Task force members Carmen Redhorse, Simon Woolridge, Marco Cruz and Michael Dance fell in behind Ethan as Michelle led the way up the trail through the woods. She was practically running as she neared the compound. They emerged into the clearing and the first thing that struck him was the silence. No children played, no one lounged in front of the camps, no groups stood around talking. "Where is everyone?" Michelle asked, looking around.

"We'll spread out and check things out," Marco said.

"I'll see if Metwater is home," Ethan said. He headed for the motor home and rapped on the door. It opened quickly. Asteria scowled at him. "If you're looking for the Prophet, he's not here," she said. "He's with the others, searching for Hunter." She frowned at Michelle. "Why did you bring the cops here? Why aren't you searching for your boy?"

Michelle shoved past Asteria, into the motor home. "Was Hunter here?" she asked. "Did you see him?"

Asteria looked confused. "What do you mean? Of course he wasn't here."

"Daniel Metwater threatened to hurt him,"

Michelle said. "He was near the shower shack before I went in. He must have seen his chance and snatched my baby to frighten me."

Asteria took a step back until she was pressed against the wall. "You need to leave," she said. "The Prophet told us you were crazy and I didn't want to believe him, but I see it's true."

Ethan put his hand on Michelle's shoulder— she practically vibrated with anger, and he was sure if he hadn't been there to hold her back she would have launched herself at Asteria. "Where is Metwater now?" he asked.

Asteria didn't take her eyes off Michelle as she answered, "He and the others are searching the woods just outside camp past the shower shack. We thought Hunter might have wandered into there—he's barely crawling, so he couldn't have gone far."

"Let's go." Ethan led Michelle toward the door. "Maybe they've found something."

That bit of hope got her moving. But when they were outside, she glanced over her shoulder, back toward the motor home. "She would lie for him," she said. "But I can't believe she would do anything to harm Hunter. She loved him."

"Maybe she really doesn't know anything."

He put a hand at her back. "Show me this shower shack."

She led him across the clearing, past a cluster of tents, to another narrow path that cut through thick underbrush. Halfway along, she stopped. "Metwater threatened me here," she said, halting a few dozen yards down the path, where trees closed in on either side. "He must have cut through the underbrush and been waiting for me."

"Did he follow you after he talked to you?" Ethan asked.

"He started walking back toward camp, but he could have turned around when he was out of sight."

They continued to a wooden hut, open at the top except for a platform, on which sat a blue plastic barrel. The door to the hut was open A bearded young man was inside, painting the walls a light blue-gray. "What are you doing?" Michelle demanded.

He stopped in mid-brushstroke. "The Prophet told me to paint in here," he said.

"Why aren't you out searching with everyone else?" she asked.

"He told me it was more important to paint."

"Were there any paint marks on the walls before you started?" Ethan asked. The young man must have been working for a while—all four walls were mostly coated with paint.

The man scratched his head. "I don't know. I didn't pay any attention. Anyway, I'm almost finished."

Ethan nudged Michelle. "Let's find Metwater," he said. He could hear voices now, perhaps a sign the searchers were nearby.

"That's the same color paint that was dumped on me," she said. "Metwater must have ordered it painted to hide the evidence."

"Maybe." The voices grew louder and they emerged into a second clearing, this one empty of dwellings, but full of people. Ethan spotted Metwater right away—with his long, dark hair and all-white clothing, he stood out amidst his ragtag group of followers. "Metwater, I want to talk to you," he called.

Metwater raised his head and fixed his gaze first on Michelle. Ethan couldn't read his expression. When his gaze shifted to Ethan, Metwater looked calm—too calm. "I understand a child went missing from camp," Ethan said as he and Michelle approached the self-appointed Prophet.

"His mother reported him missing," Metwater said. "We haven't found any sign of foul play—and no sign of the child."

"He's missing because you took him," Michelle said.

Metwater turned away from her to address Ethan. "Officer, could I have a word with you? In private?"

"You'll be all right here for a moment, won't you?" Ethan asked Michelle.

She gave a stiff nod, then looked away.

He walked a short distance away with Metwater. "This is far enough," Ethan said, turning so that he could keep an eye on Michelle. She looked very vulnerable and alone standing there, arms folded and shoulders hunched, hair falling forward to hide her face.

"I'm guessing she came to you with a wild story about my having kidnapped her child," Metwater said.

Ethan said nothing.

Metwater sighed. "I don't blame Starfall," he said. "She's had a very hard time of it since her partner left. She's not well liked in camp, though I've done my best to make her feel a part of the Family. Some people simply aren't emotionally equipped for bonding."

"What are you getting at?" Ethan gave him a hard look. "You don't think her son is missing?"

"Hunter isn't here," Metwater said. "But I

don't think any of our members are responsible for his disappearance. I'm certainly not."

"What do you think happened?" Ethan asked.

"I think Starfall hid the child away to draw attention to herself and to make trouble for me."

Michelle's distress over her son hadn't been faked; Ethan was sure of it. No one was that cold. "What makes you say that?" he asked.

"I told you, she has been under a lot of strain. All these wild fantasies about me harming her or the child." He spread his arms wide. "I live in a camp full of women and children and I've never laid a hand on any of them. Why would I? What would I gain from harming any one of them?"

If Ethan could discover the answer to that question, he would be one step closer to the truth. "She says you have a locket that belonged to her late foster sister," he said.

Metwater's expression hardened. "She's a liar, Officer. Spend enough time with her and you'll learn that."

"We'll talk more later," Ethan said, and moved back to Michelle's side. The raw hope in her eyes at his approach sent a physical ache through him. He would have given a lot to be able to share good news with her at that moment. "I'm sorry," he said. "He says he doesn't know anything."

"He hasn't had time to take Hunter very far away," she said. "He must be somewhere nearby. Maybe someone is hiding him in one of the trailers. We should look now, while everyone is gone." She moved past him, headed back down the path toward camp. But she had taken only a few steps when a clamor rose behind them.

Together they turned to see a tall, barechested man with red hair running toward Metwater, something in his hand. He showed Metwater the item and they exchanged a few words. Then Metwater turned and motioned Ethan and Michelle over.

"What have you found?" Ethan asked.

"It's a child's sock." Metwater turned to the redhead. "Show him, Eugene."

Eugene opened his hand to reveal a small white sock—white except for a reddish brown stain dampening the heel.

"That looks like Hunter's sock," Michelle said. "The one he was wearing." She reached for it, but Ethan stopped her. "Where did you find that?" he asked Eugene.

"Not far. I can show you."

"What's that on the heel?" Michelle asked. She leaned forward for a closer look.

"I believe it's blood," Metwater said. "Very fresh, and quite a lot of it."

Ethan wanted to throttle him for taking such pleasure in shocking Michelle. But he didn't have time for that now. "We don't know what it is right now," he said. "Or where it came from. It might not even belong to Hunter."

But his words were too late to provide any comfort. Michelle blanched dead white, and with a keening wail she slumped to the ground.

Chapter Five

Michelle was making a habit of waking up in Ethan's arms. Under other circumstances, it wouldn't be a bad way to return to consciousness. But before she had time to enjoy the pleasant sensation of being cradled in his strength, the memory of that bloody sock flooded back, and she had to bite the inside of her cheek to keep from wailing.

"Take it easy," he said, supporting her into a sitting position. She was on the ground, Ethan beside her and people standing all around her. She recognized people from the camp, as well as some of the officers who had come into camp with them.

"I'm fine," she said. She had to be. She had to keep it together for Hunter. Gripping Ethan's arm, she pushed herself to her feet. "I want to see where they found that sock."

She thought Ethan might argue with her, but instead, he turned to Eugene. "Show us where you found it," he said.

"Uh, sure. Over here." Eugene led the way and half the camp fell in alongside them, including Metwater.

"You people all have to stay back!" one of the officers—the good-looking Hispanic guy named Marco—said. He and the other two men—Simon and Michael—herded the crowd back. Ethan, Michelle and Metwater kept following Eugene, who stopped in a brushy area maybe one hundred yards from the edge of camp. The ground all around them was trampled and dusty.

"It was hanging on a branch here," Eugene said. "Or anyways, really near here. I didn't mark the exact place."

Ethan knelt and examined the ground. "No sign of blood anywhere around here," he said. He stood and took out an evidence bag, dropped the sock in and labeled it.

Michelle longed to hold that sock, to cradle it in her hand, to put her nose to it and see if her son's scent still lingered. But she couldn't do that. That little sock was evidence now. But evidence of what? She refused to let herself dwell on the possible answers to that question.

Marco and Carmen joined them. "We need to get these people out of here and get a crime scene team in here," Carmen said.

"And we need to conduct our own search for the missing boy," Ethan said. "Starting with the camp."

"I can't allow you to search our homes without a warrant," Metwater said.

"We're talking about a missing baby," Ethan said. "If you don't want to cooperate, I promise you we can get a warrant."

"What are you hiding, Metwater?" Marco asked.

"You're wasting your time," Metwater said. "While you're conducting a useless and intrusive search of the camp, the real kidnapper will be getting away."

"So you're willing to admit now that Michelle's son is missing?" Ethan asked.

"Is that what she told you her name was? Are you sure that's not another lie?"

Michelle didn't know if she had ever hated another man as much as she hated Daniel Metwater at this moment. The power of her rage frightened her. "You're one to talk of lies," she said. "Your whole life is a lie. All these people think you're some great spiritual teacher, but I know the truth."

Something flashed in Metwater's eyes—something very like fear. But the expression was quickly masked. "You will leave this camp at once," he said. "You are no longer welcome here."

"I won't leave without my son."

Ethan put a hand on her shoulder. "Let's go back to your tent," he said. "You can wait there while we search."

"I want to help search," she said.

"The best thing is for you to wait," he said. "I know it's hard, but I promise we'll let you know as soon as we find anything."

She waited until they were at her tent before she spoke again. "My name really is Michelle," she said. "I have my birth certificate. And my driver's license. I can show you."

"You don't have to show me," he said. "I believe you."

She had to look away then, afraid he would see in her eyes how much his words meant to her. She cleared her throat. "What are you going to do while I wait?"

"One of our team members has a dog who's trained in search and rescue," he said. "We'll get him out here and hope they can pick up a trail."

She looked around the tent, at the empty

crib, the box of diapers, the baby blanket draped across the end of her cot. "I feel so helpless," she said.

"Do you want me to call someone to stay with you?" he asked.

"No. I'd rather be alone. I'm used to it."

He put his hand on her shoulder again, and she gave in to the urge to rest her cheek against it, for just a moment. Then she remembered who this was—a cop she scarcely knew—and she straightened and stepped away. "I'll be all right," she said. "Go—and find my baby."

When he was gone, she sank onto the cot and picked up the baby blanket. *Hunter, don't be scared, baby. Mommy is going to find you.*

"IF THERE WAS a scent here, I know she'd find it, but the scene is too compromised." Customs and Border Patrol Agent Randall Knightbridge stroked the neck of his Belgian Malinois, Lotte, who sat by his side, panting heavily. The dog and Randall had spent the last hour carefully searching the area from Michelle's tent to the shower shack to the place where the sock had been found. Lotte had alerted a few times, but every time the trail petered out after only a few yards.

"Thanks for trying." Ethan gave the dog

a pat and surveyed the stretch of trampled ground extending fifty yards or more past the general boundaries of Daniel Metwater's camp. "No sign of blood, either, so I guess that's a good thing."

"Lotte definitely would have picked up any human blood," Randall said. "People walking over that wouldn't hide the scent from her nose."

Carmen, Michael and Marco joined them. "We searched the last of the tents and trailers," Michael said. "No sign of the missing kid."

"We found a few illegal drugs and some questionable IDs, but no sign of an out-of-place toddler," Carmen said. "For what it's worth, most people seem pretty upset about Hunter's disappearance."

"Nobody is offering up any clues to what happened, though," Marco said. "No one else was around the shower this morning."

"No one will admit to hearing Metwater threaten Starfall or her baby," Michael said.

"Her name is Michelle," Ethan said. "She only used Starfall so Metwater wouldn't realize she's related to a woman his brother was dating, who died under mysterious circumstances."

"If Metwater took the child, he got him out

of here in a hurry," Marco said. "How much time do you estimate passed between when Starfall—I mean Michelle—discovered him missing and we got here?"

"About two hours," Ethan said. "Plenty of time to give the kid to someone else to hide."

"Or to kill him and bury the body," Michael said, his expression grim.

"We need to get the blood on that sock tested," Ethan said.

"I'll take it to the lab this evening," Carmen said. "Meanwhile, what are we going to do about Michelle?"

"I don't think it's safe for her to stay here," Ethan said. "Metwater already beat her up once."

"He kicked her out, didn't he?" Michael asked. "Does she have any family or friends in town she can stay with?"

"I don't think so," Ethan said.

"We can try to find a place for her at the women's shelter," Carmen said. "Though they're usually pretty full."

"The other half of my duplex is vacant," Ethan said. "Maybe she could stay there."

"If she could put up with having you for a neighbor," Michael said.

Carmen looked thoughtful. "It might not be

a bad idea. She'd be safe, but close by if we needed her."

And she wouldn't have to be alone, Ethan thought. The emptiness in her voice when she had told him she was used to being by herself pulled at something deep inside him. She might be hard and a little prickly, but he figured she had her reasons. He might not be able to bring her son back to her tonight, but he could show her he was on her side.

The other Rangers headed to their vehicles, and he made his way to Michelle's tent. "Hello?" he called at the door.

"Come in."

He lifted the flap and stepped inside. For a primitive dwelling, the women had made it as comfortable as possible, with rugs on the floor and colorful blankets draped over the cots and camp chairs. A suitcase lay open on Michelle's cot, and she was folding clothes into it. At his approach, she turned to him, the longing in her eyes so raw it made his throat tighten, hurting for her. "I don't have any news for you yet," he said. "But we didn't find any signs of violence." Which didn't mean there hadn't been any, but he wanted to offer her what comfort he could.

She looked down at the suitcase and picked

up a tiny shirt. "I was just packing a few things—my clothes, but Hunter's, too. I'll have to come back later for the crib and other stuff. He'll need them when you find him."

When you find him. He hoped he could live up to that trust. "You can't stay here," he said.

"No. I have a little money saved. I'll get a cheap motel room in town." She closed the suitcase and zipped it shut. Her hair fell forward, revealing the pale skin at the back of her neck. He had to fight the urge to bend down and inhale the scent of her there, to run his fingers over the soft flesh. She was such an enticing combination of satin and steel—so strong and yet so vulnerable. "Could I come to Ranger Headquarters during the day—just to be close if anything does happen?" she asked. "I don't think I could bear sitting in a motel room all day, not knowing what was going on."

"Of course," he said. "But you don't need the motel room. I have a safe place for you to stay."

Her eyebrows pulled closer together and her lips thinned. "Where?"

"I live in a duplex near the national park. The other half is empty right now. The property is owned by the federal government. You can stay there. You'll be safe and close—and Metwater will never think to look for you there."

Her expression relaxed. "I'd like that. Thank you."

He picked up her suitcase. "Let's go. We'll send for the rest of your stuff later."

"All this gentlemanly behavior is going to go to my head," she said. "I'm not used to it."

They left the tent and started across the fire ring. They had only taken a few steps when Metwater stepped out of his motor home. "Starfall!"

Ethan was probably the only one to notice her flinch at the sound of Metwater's voice. The hard expression on her face gave nothing away as she turned toward him. "I don't have anything else to say to you," she said.

"But I have something to say to you." His long strides quickly closed the gap between them. He held out his hand. "Give me the keys to the car."

She lifted her chin and looked him in the eye. "What car?"

"The one you've been driving. It belongs to me."

"It does not! I never signed your stupid agreement to hand over all my worldly goods."

"No. I'll have to speak to Asteria about that oversight."

"She didn't have anything to do with it," Michelle said. "I simply never turned them in."

"It doesn't matter." He smiled, a look that might have charmed under other circumstances. "Greg signed the papers—the car was in his name."

"No." She shook her head, curls dancing. "That car is mine. Greg gave it to me when he left. It's the only thing he ever did give me, the bum."

"It wasn't his to give," Metwater said. "He had already relinquished the title to me. I can show you the paperwork, if you don't believe me."

"You're going to take her car?" Ethan asked. "Why?"

Metwater shifted his gaze to Ethan, the sneer still firmly in place. "Because it isn't her car. The Family is a cooperative group. When a new member joins, she signs over all her possessions for the use of the group. We believe in negating the self for the good of the whole."

"You said the car belonged to you, not the group," Ethan said.

"I am the guardian of my family's possessions."

"It's just another scam," Michelle said. "Everyone else may not see through it, but I do."

Metwater looked at her again. "You should be careful what you say," he said. "Especially in front of a police officer." He turned to Ethan. "If you look into her background, Officer, I think you'll find she's far from innocent."

"He doesn't know what he's talking about," Michelle said. She opened her purse and pulled out the car keys. "Take it. It's not worth anything, anyway." She hurled the keys into the dirt at his feet and turned away. "Let's get out of here."

"Don't pretend you don't know what I'm talking about," Metwater called after her. "Or have you already forgotten Madeline Perry?"

Michelle faltered and swayed. Before Ethan had time to react, Metwater delivered his parting shot. "This isn't the first child you were responsible for who disappeared, is it?"

Chapter Six

When Michelle started moving again, she ran. Ethan glared at Metwater, then hurried after her. He found her waiting by the passenger door of his cruiser. He unlocked it and she climbed in. "Let's get out of here," she said.

He stowed her suitcase in the back, then slid into the driver's seat. He waited for her to explain Metwater's accusation—to tell him who Madeline Perry was. But she only stared out the side window, fists clenched, back stiff. If he tried to question her now, it would only come across like an interrogation. He would have to wait until she was ready.

By the time he parked the cruiser at the curb in front of the duplex, her refusal to speak made the air seem heavier and harder to breathe. He retrieved her suitcase from the back and led the way up the walk. She followed a few steps behind him.

He unlocked the door and opened it. "It's furnished, so you should have everything you need," he said. "We keep the kitchen and bathroom stocked with the basics, in case any visiting officials need to use it."

She took the suitcase from his fingers and moved past him, inside. His resolve broke and he blurted, "Do you want to tell me what Metwater was talking about?"

She turned to face him, her eyes empty, her expression bleak. "You're a cop," she said as she started to close the door. "You figure it out."

He stood on the stoop, staring at the closed door for several seconds, debating whether to beat on the wood and demand to settle this now, or wait until morning when he hoped she would have cooled off.

He settled for walking next door to his half of the house and going straight to his computer. A search with the keywords *Michelle Munson* and *Madeline Perry* turned up more than one hundred hits. He hunched forward to read the first one, a decade-old article from the *Chicago Tribune*.

"A confidential source in the district attorney's office has identified the chief suspect in six-year-old Madeline Perry's disappearance as her sixteen-year-old babysitter. Though the source declined to divulge the name of the suspect, against whom charges are expected to be brought shortly, the original report of Madeline's disappearance was made by sixteen-year-old Michelle Munson, who is identified in the original police report as the child's babysitter. Miss Munson is the foster child of Phillip and Georgia Little, next-door neighbors to the Perrys. Others in the neighborhood describe Miss Munson as 'a very troubled young woman.'"

ETHAN READ MORE newspaper articles, which described the disappearance of six-year-old Madeline from her parents' backyard on a Tuesday afternoon in June. The babysitter, Michelle Munson, reported that she had gone inside to prepare a snack for Madeline, who was swinging on her play set, and when she returned ten minutes later, the child was gone. She searched the area for half an hour before calling the police.

Story after story painted Michelle as a child who had been abandoned by her mother at around age ten, who had lived in a series of foster homes since that time, and had reportedly spent time in a juvenile detention center after being caught shoplifting. She had reportedly been very jealous of Madeline's home and possessions, often commenting on how nice the child's clothes were and how she wished she could live in a house like hers with parents like hers. The implication in most of the articles was that Michelle had killed Madeline and hidden the body in an attempt to take her place in the Perry household.

A fuzzy black-and-white photograph that accompanied one article showed a slight girl with a mass of dark curls, dressed in an ill-fitting jumpsuit, being escorted into court by two uniformed guards.

Ethan read faster, searching for an article that reported on the trial and its results. He found nothing about the trial, but a front-page story from November of that year reported what the paper termed "a startling development." Madeline Perry had been found alive and well in Mexico City, living with her mother, who had divorced her father two years' prior and lost custody of the girl in a heated court battle. Madeline and her mother both confirmed that Michelle Munson had nothing to do with Madeline's disappearance. Instead, her mother had been watching the house for days, waiting for her chance to grab her daughter and run.

Ethan sat back in his chair, drained. For almost six months sixteen-year-old Michelle had lived in hell, accused of the most horrible crime—killing a child—with no family, no friends, no one on her side. In the end, she was exonerated, but by then she had lost everything. He could find nothing about what had happened to her after Madeline was found. Certainly none of the papers printed apologies, and as far as he could determine, no one stepped forward to help the girl.

Anger, raw and searing, filled him. How could someone have let this happen? No wonder Michelle had built such a tough shell around herself—she had had to in order to survive.

And why was Metwater bringing it up now? Did he really think this story was going to make Ethan less sympathetic toward Michelle? Was the fact that she had been falsely accused before supposed to lead the Rangers to believe she was guilty now?

He thought of her now, separated from him only by a wall, but perhaps more alone than she had ever been. Her child was missing and she had no one to lean on. No one to comfort her.

Except him. He wouldn't let her go through this alone—not when she had suffered so much already.

He went next door and knocked. When she didn't answer, he knocked again.

"Go away," she called through the door.

"No."

He waited, scarcely daring to breathe. He had raised his hand to knock again when the door opened. She was pale, her eyes swollen and red-rimmed. "What do you want?" she asked.

"I know about Madeline Perry," he said. "I read the news articles online. I'm so sorry you had to go through that."

"I don't need your pity." She started to close the door again, but he shot his hand out, stopping her.

"I'm not pitying you," he said. "I'm angry that you had to go through that."

She studied his face as if weighing the sincerity of his words. "If you're angry, I guess that makes two of us," she said.

"Does that mean you'll let me in?" he asked.

She took hold of the front of his shirt and pulled his face down to hers, her lips pressed to his in an urgent kiss that sent heat crackling through him. Before he even had time to respond, she drew away again. "Yes," she said, and tugged him inside.

MICHELLE'S LIFE HAD become a nightmare from which she couldn't wake. She was being carried along in a flood, out of control. That a man who was a cop—a profession that had never been kind to her—would be the one steady thing she could hold on to didn't make sense to her. But nothing made sense these days.

A hard life had taught her that the only way to cope when the worst you could imagine had happened was to focus on right now—you got through this moment, and then the next, and then the next. Anticipating the future was too frightening, and dwelling on the past too sad.

Right now, in this moment, she was with the one person who believed in her. She wanted to hang on to the moment, to prolong it as long as possible. As soon as the door shut behind him, she pulled Ethan to her once more and kissed him again. She arched her back and pressed her body to his, reveling in the hard plane of his chest and the firm hold of his hands as he angled his mouth against hers and returned the kiss.

Ethan's tongue swept across her lips, a sensual invitation to deepen the contact. She opened to him, wanting to be closer, to learn his secrets and perhaps to share a few of her own. She caressed his back, the muscles shifting at her touch, then brought her hands around to his chest, to fumble at the buttons of his shirt.

He captured her hand in his and broke the kiss. "What are you doing?" he asked, his voice husky, his eyes glazed with passion.

"I'm taking off your clothes," she said, undoing another button. "Feel free to help."

"I don't think that's a good idea," he said.

"No? You kissed me as if you thought it was a very good idea."

"You're a crime victim. I'm supposed to be looking out for you, not taking advantage of you."

She turned her attention from the buttons to his face. "That is so touchingly noble and ethical, Officer Do-Right," she said. "But do I look like a woman who's being taken advantage of?"

He ran his tongue over his bottom lip. Did he have any idea how sexy he looked, all noble and indecisive? She placed one finger on that same bottom lip. "Answer the question, Officer."

"You look like a strong, sexy woman who knows what she wants," he said.

"Good answer. And what I want right now is you."

He didn't waste any more time talking, but gathered her into his arms and kissed her until she was breathless. No more Mr. Indecision, he led her toward the bedroom, which held a chair, dresser and most important for their purposes—a made-up queen-size bed. Eyes locked to hers, he removed his utility belt and draped it over the back of the chair, then finished undoing the buttons on his shirt and removed it to reveal a muscular chest lightly dusted with brown hair. Her breath caught at the sight, and her knees felt wobbly.

He took her in his arms again. "You're sure this is what you want?" he asked.

"I need this," she said. "I need to not think about things, to just be with someone who isn't judging me or expecting anything from me."

"I'm not judging or expecting." He stroked her hair back from her face. "I just want to be with you."

She grabbed the hem of her shirt and tugged it over her head, then pushed down her skirt, leaving her standing before him in her panties and bra. She wasn't worried about what he might see—she had earned every stretch mark and blemish honestly, and she knew enough about sex by now to understand that the physical was only a small part of what made an encounter good.

In any case, the smile on his face, and the way he caressed her hips and kissed the valley of her cleavage, let her know he liked what he saw. She pulled him toward the bed and they fell together on it, already entwined, learning the shape and feel of each other. All his earlier hesitancy was gone—he matched her move for move, teasing her and thrilling her, replacing her pain and sadness, at least momentarily, with an awareness of her body and the pleasure it could both give and receive.

He patted her hip and kissed the tip of her nose. "I have to take care of one thing," he said. "Be right back."

He rose and went into the bathroom. She propped herself up on one elbow and enjoyed the view of him, naked, walking away from her. This was one cop who definitely kept in shape.

He returned quickly, a foil packet in one hand. She collapsed back on the pillows, surprised into laughter. "When you told me the place was furnished, I didn't think you meant *everything.*"

He unwrapped the condom and rolled it on. "Officers on temporary assignment or special guests sometimes stay here, so we try to keep it stocked with whatever we think they might need."

"Guess you take that motto to *protect* and serve seriously," she teased.

"Oh, yeah." He knelt over her, parting her legs with one knee. "Though sometimes it's more of a pleasure than a duty."

She slid her hands up his arms to thread her fingers through the hair at the back of his head. "I'm ready to be served, Officer."

He slid into her and began to move, and she lost the power of speech. Forget her plan to keep him waiting and call the shots—his skilled mouth and hands and sex had her surrendering to him, losing herself to sensation and passion. He leaned down and kissed her closed eyelids, and whispered in her ear. "You don't have to do anything," he said. "Just let go."

His voice, deep and hypnotic, and the words he spoke, so full of tenderness and caring, acted as a soothing balm to her frayed nerves and frantic mind. She did as he said and let go, floating on waves of sensation, climbing higher toward a breathless release that made her cry out with joy.

His own cries soon joined hers as his climax shuddered through them both. She clung to him as he slid out of her and settled beside her, his head on her breast. She stroked his hair, her eyes still closed, clinging to that brief moment of bliss.

"That was...intense," he said after a long moment.

"Mmm-hmm." She snuggled closer, and he wrapped his arms around her. She wanted to ride this wave of pleasure right into sleep—to shut worry and fear out for a little while longer.

But her brain wasn't going to allow it. As the afterglow faded, the reality of what was happening to her rushed back with the impact of a sucker punch. She rolled over to face Ethan. "How did Metwater find out about Madeline?" she asked.

"Probably the same way I did—I searched online for your name and hers."

"He wasn't supposed to know my real name."

"Maybe Asteria searched your things and found out for him."

She lay back down, her head nestled in the hollow of his shoulder. "Maybe." The idea hurt more than she cared to admit. She had thought Asteria was her friend.

"That must have been horrible for you, when Madeline disappeared," he said.

She had never talked about that time with anyone—mostly because there had never been anyone to talk to—no one who cared enough to ask. "At first I was terrified something terrible had happened to her," she said. "She was a really sweet little girl, and the two of us had gotten close. But it didn't take long to realize that everyone was blaming me. After all, I was the kid with no family. I'd already been in trouble with the law."

"What about your foster parents?" he asked. "Didn't they defend you?"

"When people first started saying I had hurt Madeline, the Littles couldn't distance themselves from me fast enough. They called my caseworker and insisted I be removed from their home. I was a bad influence on their other children. So I ended up back in a group home. At least, until they sent me to jail." She shuddered at the memory.

He caressed her shoulder. "I can't believe no one thought to look at the mother. So many child abductions are carried out by the noncustodial parent."

"They thought they had found their guilty party in me, so they didn't need to look any closer. They wanted the quick and easy solution, to make a splash in the papers."

"But you were exonerated. I don't understand why Metwater even brought it up."

"Because he hates me. And he wants you to doubt me. Sometimes that little seed of doubt it all it takes." She braced herself, waiting for his answer. Maybe Metwater's plan had worked. Maybe Ethan—despite the intimacy they had just shared—*did* have doubts about her innocence or her sanity or her trustworthiness. He wouldn't be the first.

"I don't doubt you," he said. "And I don't trust anything Metwater says. Why does he hate you?"

"Some people would say I'm an easy person to hate." At least if people didn't like you, they usually left you alone. Maybe that wasn't the healthiest way to get through life, but it had worked for her so far.

"Don't say that," he said. "It's not true."

She raised herself up to look down on him. "How do you know? You hardly know me."

"I know you're a survivor. You're a good mother. You're smart."

He thought she was smart? The idea sent

a flutter through her heart and she lay down again, not wanting him to read her agitation in her expression. "Maybe he hates me because he knows I'm right about his brother," she said. "David did murder Cass."

"Or maybe it's more than that," Ethan said. "Maybe he thinks you know what his brother was involved in."

"I've wondered about that. Whatever it was, maybe Daniel was involved, too. Maybe it had something to do with the Russian mob. They ended up killing David, so maybe Daniel is afraid they'll come after him, too, if word gets out. That would be enough to make him hate me."

"I'd love to know what David was doing that worried your sister," Ethan said.

"Me, too. I was hoping if I stuck around Metwater's *family* long enough I could find out."

"We'll find out," Ethan said. "But later. Right now we need to find Hunter."

The mention of her son was like an arrow to her heart, the pain she had been fighting off for the last hour returning tenfold. She struggled to take a deep breath. She had been strong for so long, but was she really strong enough to get through this? Not alone.

"Will you stay here with me tonight?" she asked, hoping she didn't sound desperate. If he said no, she wouldn't beg, no matter how much she wanted to.

He gathered her close and kissed her forehead. "Just try and make me leave."

ETHAN WOKE TO gray light in an unfamiliar room, unease heavy in his chest. Then he identified the sound that had woken him—muffled sobbing from the woman beside him.

Michelle lay on her side, her back to him, curled into herself, the blanket pulled over her head. The choking, wrenching sobs made his chest hurt, and his first instinct was to pretend he didn't hear and find a way to slip out of bed and escape into the bathroom.

But that was the coward's way out, and he wasn't a coward. So instead, he reached out and pulled her to him, and kissed the top of her head and held her tightly. "I'm right here," he said. "I won't leave."

"I never cry," she sobbed, bunching the sheet in her fists. "I hate crying, but I can't help myself. Hunter—" A fresh wave of tears washed away whatever else she might have said.

"I can't even imagine how hard it is," he said. "It's like someone has cut out part of my heart. I would rather they had hurt me than to have taken him." She buried her face against him and sobbed until her tears wet his shoulder and his arms ached from holding her trembling body. Lovemaking had breached the barrier between them, but this was a deeper kind of intimacy.

At last the sobbing subsided. She sat up, wiping at her eyes. "Thank you," she said. "I doubt your job description includes dealing with weeping women."

"You might be surprised." But was that really how she thought of him—as a cop first? Even after the closeness they had shared last night, she still didn't trust him. She didn't trust his badge.

"I'm going to take a shower," she said.

"I'll make coffee."

He dressed and moved to the kitchen, where he found the makings for coffee, but not much else. They'd have to stop by the store sometime today and get some food. He was waiting for the coffee to finish dripping through the brewer when his cell phone chimed. He fished the phone out of his pocket and saw he had a text from Carmen. A glance at the clock showed a little past seven. She was up early.

He was reading the text when Michelle came

in, dressed in fresh jeans and a T-shirt, her hair still wet from the shower. "What's wrong?" she asked. "You look upset."

"I just got a text from Carmen. They got the results back from the lab on the sock Eugene found."

She clutched the counter and sucked in a deep breath. "What are the results?"

"I don't know." He pocketed the phone. "The commander wants us both at headquarters at eight o'clock."

Chapter Seven

Michelle barely managed to choke down the cup of coffee Ethan handed her. The fact that the Rangers wanted her at their headquarters, to deliver the test results in person, had to be a bad sign, right? She didn't ask Ethan—she didn't want him to confirm her suspicions. Neither of them said anything until they were almost to Black Canyon of the Gunnison National Park, where the Ranger Brigade had their headquarters, and then he reached over and took her hand, surprising her.

"Whatever the test results, don't give up hope," he said.

She cleared her throat. "Having a baby is all about hope," she said. "I never had any before I had Hunter."

He squeezed her hand. "We're going to find him."

"I know you'll try." That was more than anyone else had done for her in years. More, really, than she had done for herself. She had told herself she was hiding out with Daniel Metwater's group in order to prove Cass didn't overdose on drugs, but really, living with a reclusive group that didn't require her to have a job or interact with the rest of society had been a kind of cop-out. Things would have to be different once they found Hunter. She'd have to find a place to live and a job and start to give him the kind of stable, normal life she had always longed for.

She thought she had calmed down a little by the time they arrived at Ranger Brigade Headquarters, but her heart started racing again when she and Ethan were greeted by no fewer than six of the Rangers, including the commander. "I'm Commander Graham Ellison," he introduced himself. He had a firm handshake, a stern expression and closely cropped graying hair that made her think of army drill sergeants in the movies.

"What's going on, Commander?" Ethan asked.

"That's what we're trying to find out," Ellison said. He motioned to a rolling chair someone had pulled to the center of the room. "Ms. Munson, sit down, please."

She didn't like the way he ordered her to sit—albeit politely—instead of asking if she would like to sit, but she really didn't have a choice. She doubted her shaking legs would support her much longer. "Just tell me what the results were of the blood test on Hunter's sock," she said as she lowered herself into the chair. "Is it his blood?"

"It isn't." Carmen rolled a chair over to sit beside Michelle. "It wasn't even human blood. The lab said it's from an animal—most likely rabbit."

"Rabbit?" Had she heard right? Relief flooded her at the knowledge that it wasn't Hunter's blood staining the sock, but rabbit? "I don't understand."

"Someone is trying to play games with us," Commander Ellison said. He moved to stand in front of her, fixing her with the stern gaze she associated with principals and prison guards. "Is it you?"

"No!" She sought Ethan's face in the crowd of officers gathered around her. "What are you accusing me of?"

"Daniel Metwater seems to think you've set up some kind of hoax to draw attention to yourself," the commander said. "If you have, I promise there will be serious consequences."

"This isn't a hoax." Ethan stepped forward. "Her son is missing and she didn't have anything to do with it."

"Metwater is trying to make me look bad in order to divert suspicion from himself," she said.

Ellison scowled as if weighing the merits of her claims. She fought not to shrink under his gaze. Ethan believed her, but maybe he was the only one.

Ethan rested his hand on her shoulder, steadying her. "Michelle isn't guilty of anything but making an enemy of Daniel Metwater," he said. "But there is something you need to know." He looked at her. "It's bound to come out sooner rather than later, especially if Metwater is talking about it."

Yes, Metwater would make sure everyone knew about Madeline Perry. Michelle sighed, then lifted her head and looked the commander in the eye. "When I was sixteen, a child I was babysitting disappeared," she said. "I was arrested and charged with her murder, after a bloody handkerchief with her blood on it was found in my coat pocket." She told them the whole story—that the handkerchief was from a nosebleed Madeline had had that morning, about the DA and police chief who wanted to make a name for themselves by closing the case quickly—and about the foster child with no family to speak for her, whom no one would believe because she already had a record for shoplifting an expensive blouse and a necklace from a clothing store she couldn't afford to shop at.

"I was in a juvenile facility, awaiting trial, when a family friend spotted Madeline with her mother in Mexico," she said. "They released me without an apology. I had no one to go to, until Cass's family heard the story somehow. They took me in, and Cass became the sister I never had. She's the only reason I ended up with Metwater's group. Now that he knows I know the truth about Cass's death, he wants to get rid of me, and he'll do whatever he can to make that happen."

She braced herself for what she was sure would come next—the suspicious looks and halfhearted expressions of sympathy. Instead, Carmen leaned over and took her hand. The other woman—a cop, Michelle reminded herself—had tears in her eyes. "What a nightmare to have to live through," she said.

"Thank you for telling us about this," the

commander said. "I'm sure it wasn't easy. But it could help us. Whoever is responsible for your son's disappearance may be using this incident from your past to throw suspicion on you or frighten you into silence."

"Daniel Metwater has motive and opportunity," Ethan said.

"The search of his motor home didn't turn up any evidence," Marco said. "And no one we talked to reported ever seeing him with the boy. In fact, no one saw the boy this morning."

"There aren't that many people in the camp," Carmen said. "If Metwater chose his time right—when people were occupied with chores—it might be possible to avoid seeing anyone."

"Or his followers might be reluctant to snitch on their Prophet," Michael said.

"I think we need to lean on Andi Matheson," Ethan said. "She's closest to Metwater. They practically live together."

"Andi is eight months pregnant," Simon said. "We won't win any friends if it looks like we're bullying her."

"We won't bully her," Michael said. "We'll simply encourage her to tell the truth about Metwater. We'll offer her our protection."

"She won't tell you anything," Simon said,

his expression sour. "She thinks Metwater hung the moon and stars."

"She may look loyal on the outside, but I think she's getting a little disillusioned with the Prophet," Michelle said.

The others looked at her as if they had momentarily forgotten she was there. "Asteria doesn't just worship Metwater," she said. "She's in love with him. But he doesn't feel the same way about her. He doesn't make any secret of sleeping with other women."

"We could use that to persuade her to cooperate with us," Marco said.

"You don't have to trick her," Michelle said. "Just remind her that you're trying to find Hunter. She loves him and she's probably worried about him. She won't want to think Metwater had anything to do with his disappearance, but if she knows anything, her love for Hunter will win out over her infatuation with Metwater, I think."

"I'll go with you to interview her," Simon said.

"I want to go, too." Michelle stood. "I need to get my trunk and some of Hunter's things I left behind." She could see Simon was about to object, so she added, "She'll be more likely to cooperate with you if she sees that I trust you."

In the end, Ethan and Simon traveled in one car, while Michelle ended up riding with Carmen. Michelle was more comfortable around the other woman than she had been previously, but she still didn't completely trust her.

"Jake says hello," Carmen said as they headed toward the turnoff for Metwater's compound. "He has his Fish and Wildlife agents on the lookout for Hunter."

Jake Lohmiller, Carmen's fiancé, was the Fish and Wildlife agent Michelle had tried to scam—and yes, had flirted with—when he first came to the area. Knowing he and Carmen had discussed her made Michelle want to squirm in her seat. "I'm surprised he would want to help me," she said.

"He likes strong women. He always said it's one reason he ended up with me."

"Yeah, well, you didn't try to extort money out of him."

Carmen laughed. "It served him right. I still give him a hard time about losing his badge. What kind of cop does that?"

Michelle wondered if she had slipped into an alternate dimension—one in which the cops were nice, people believed her and she didn't feel the need to always try to game every situation.

If only Hunter were here with her, she might even grow to like this version of reality.

She followed the officers down the trail into camp from the parking lot. Suddenly, the place she had called home for the past few months felt threatening. The people gathered outside the tents and trailers stared openly, but she knew just as many others watched from behind cover. Some of them would be angry, feeling she had betrayed the Family by bringing the police into their lives. Many would wonder what had happened to Hunter—and if she had anything to do with his disappearance.

Ethan moved up beside her. "Simon and Carmen and I are going to interview Asteria," he said. "Will you be okay out here by yourself?"

"Of course." She had been looking after herself for more than a decade. She certainly didn't need a bodyguard. "I'll wait for you in my tent. I can finish packing up everything."

"Sounds like a plan." He patted her shoulder and, along with the other Rangers, moved toward Metwater's motor home.

Michelle headed for the white tent nearest the motor home. Greg had bought it from some hunters in Montrose. After he moved out, she had invited Asteria to live with her, since the senator's daughter didn't have a place of her own. Metwater probably claimed the tent belonged to him now. She didn't care. It wasn't as if she was ever going to live in it again. Once she and Hunter were together again, she would take her savings and make a fresh start. Maybe she'd go back to school, or start a business. She was smart and resourceful, and she didn't need anyone else to decide what she should do.

Ethan and the others had assumed Asteria was in Metwater's motor home, but she didn't spend all her time there. Maybe she was in the tent. If so, Michelle would have a chance to talk to her first. She could make her own plea for Asteria's help in finding Hunter. With a child of her own soon to be born, Asteria would be especially sympathetic to Michelle's pain. She would want to do whatever she could to help her.

Michelle quickened her pace. By the time the trio of officers was climbing the steps to Metwater's motor home, she was pushing back the flap of the white tent.

Yet again, a sense of unreality shook her. The rugs that had softened the floor and the scarves that had added color to the tent walls had vanished. The cots where she and Asteria had slept were gone, as were the chairs, tables and lamps, Hunter's crib and the baskets and bins where the women stored extra supplies.

"My trunk!" Michelle rushed into the tent, to the place at the foot of her cot where her trunk—containing all her pictures, the newspaper clippings about Cass and David Metwater she had saved and Hunter's birth certificate—had been. She turned in a slow circle, hoping to spot this precious depository for her few keepsakes, but the tent was empty, as if it had never been occupied.

She raced from the tent and up the steps to the motor home, where she beat on the door, rage blinding her to the stares of those around her. The door opened and Ethan took both her hands in his. "What is it?" he asked. "What's wrong?"

"Everything's gone," she said.

"What do you mean?" He led her into the motor home, where Metwater and Asteria stood with Carmen and Simon.

"The tent is empty. All my things—all Hunter's things. My trunk! It's all gone." She turned to Metwater. "What did you do with it all?"

"You left," Metwater said. "Asteria decided to move in with me. I redistributed the items in the tent, and disposed of whatever was no longer needed."

"That trunk was mine!" She tried to launch herself at him, but Ethan and Simon held her back.

"You're wrong," Metwater said. "Everything you had is mine now. Everything."

Chapter Eight

The stricken look in Michelle's eyes tore at Ethan. He moved between her and Metwater. "Are you talking about her son—Hunter?"

"No." He made a dismissive gesture. "I don't have Hunter. I already told you, she's a liar. You shouldn't believe anything she says."

"Maybe in this case, you're the liar," Ethan said. "It's something I intend to find out." Ignoring Metwater's glare, he turned to Asteria. "Ma'am, would you come outside with us for a moment? We need to ask you some questions."

"I can answer your questions here," she said.

"No." Carmen took her arm. "We want to talk in private."

Ethan braced himself for an argument. Asteria, like Metwater, had made no secret of her loathing for the Rangers. Judging by her stormy expression, her opinion hadn't changed.

"Go with them," Metwater said. "The sooner they find out you don't know anything, the sooner they'll leave us alone."

Lips pursed in a stubborn pout, Asteria let Carmen lead her toward the door. Ethan took Michelle's arm and tugged her after them. Outside, he released her. "We need to talk to Asteria alone," he said. "You can wait with my cruiser if you like."

"I need to find my trunk," she said.

"We're going to try to get Asteria to tell us what Metwater did with it," he said.

She didn't look happy with the answer, but she turned abruptly and walked away. He watched her leave and was struck by how slight and vulnerable she looked. Her fierce attitude often made her seem larger.

He turned and followed Carmen and Asteria into the tent. Carmen had found a folding chair for the pregnant woman to sit on. Asteria perched on the edge of the chair, eyeing the Rangers warily. Ethan remembered seeing pictures of socialite Andi Matheson in the newspaper and online. The sometimes model had dated sports figures and rock stars and had made more than one "most beautiful people" list. Now she looked listless and uncomfortable, her hair dull and skin sallow. "How are you doing?" Ethan asked. "Are you feeling all right?"

"Why do people always ask me that? I'm fine."

"You look tired," Carmen said. "Have you seen a doctor during your pregnancy?"

"That's none of your business."

So much for trying to persuade her they were on her side. "What can you tell us about Hunter and Michelle?" Ethan asked.

"I can't tell you anything," she said.

"Do you say that because you truly don't know anything, or because you're afraid of Daniel Metwater?" Carmen asked.

Something he couldn't read flickered in her eyes. "I'm not afraid of the Prophet," she said.

"You're closer to him than anyone else in this camp," Ethan said. "Maybe you can help us understand him better."

She said nothing, but he thought she didn't look as hostile. "You saw Michelle the morning Hunter disappeared, right?" he asked. "How did she look?"

"What do you mean? She looked fine."

"She says Daniel Metwater beat her when he caught her in his motor home the night before."

"The Prophet doesn't beat people." She said this in the same tone of voice she might have declared that he didn't eat pig's feet or wear polyester—as if doing so was beneath him.

"Someone hurt her, though. She was still hurting that morning."

"She had some bruises," Asteria admitted.

"How did she behave with Hunter?"

Asteria shrugged. "Normal."

"What was she doing with him?" Carmen asked.

"She was taking care of him. Cuddling him."

"So she wasn't angry with him, or distant?"

She frowned. "No. Starfall is a good mother."

"When she left your tent to go to the showers, did she take Hunter with her?" Ethan asked.

"Yes."

"Did you see her or Hunter after that?"

"I saw her when she ran back to camp looking for him."

"Where was Daniel Metwater while she was in the shower?" Ethan asked. "Did you see him?"

"I don't know."

He tried to hold her gaze and failed. She stared down at her lap, picking at a patch on her long skirt. "When was the first time you saw Daniel Metwater after Michelle headed to the shower?" Ethan asked.

"I saw him coming out of his motor home on the way to breakfast." She lifted her head, her expression defiant. "He goes to breakfast about that time every morning. There's nothing sinister about that."

"I never said there was. Did you see him anywhere else? Anywhere near the showers?"

"No. I went back into the tent and lay down." She smoothed her skirt over her belly. "I was tired."

Maybe she was telling the truth. Or maybe she was trying to protect Metwater. "You didn't see Metwater with Hunter?"

She shook her head, lips pressed tightly together as if holding back words. Time to change tactics. "Why did he take Michelle's trunk?" Ethan asked.

Asteria blinked, her blue eyes troubled. "She left and didn't take it with her."

"But she intended to come back for it," he said. "Everything in it was valuable to her—family pictures and important papers. Hunter's birth certificate was in that trunk."

Asteria shifted in the chair. "He thought it was abandoned."

"Can you help us get her things back?" Ethan asked.

She looked away. "I can't."

"Where do you keep things like pictures and personal items?" Carmen asked.

Asteria looked around the now-empty tent. "I have a lockbox. Why?"

"What if Metwater took them away from you?" Carmen asked.

"Imagine how that would feel," Ethan said.

Asteria shook her head. "He didn't take Starfall's trunk—she left it."

"What did he do with it?" Ethan asked. "Did he open it?"

"No. It was locked."

"Then you did see it." He moved in closer, leaning over her. "What happened when he couldn't open the trunk?"

"I don't know!"

"You do know something. Why are you covering up for him? It's not as if he's faithful to you."

He couldn't mistake the hurt in her eyes at that remark, but he pressed on. "If Daniel Metwater would take a woman's most precious possessions, how do you know he didn't take her child, too?" he asked.

"He didn't. He wouldn't."

"Help us find Hunter, Andi. He needs his mother."

Tears streamed down her pale cheeks. "I don't know anything about Hunter," she whispered.

"What about the trunk?" Carmen asked.

She bowed her head. "He had a couple of guys haul it off. He told them to destroy it."

"Who?" Ethan asked.

"Eugene and Derek. I don't know what they did with it. I really don't!"

"Where can we find Eugene and Derek?" Ethan asked.

She shook her head, mute.

Ethan turned away. The job was supposed to make him tough enough to ignore a woman's tears, but he wasn't there yet. "You can go now," he said. "Thank you for your help."

She jumped up and hurried away. Carmen moved past Ethan. "I'll start looking for Eugene and Derek, but my guess is we're not going to find that trunk."

"Maybe we'll get lucky," he said.

But luck wasn't on their side. No one in camp had seen Eugene or Derek that morning. Ethan suspected at least some of them were lying, but pressing the issue wasn't getting them anywhere. "I'll break the news to Michelle," he said. "We've got a chopper coming in this afternoon to do an aerial search for Hunter."

"I hope the little guy is all right," Carmen said. "Even though I don't care for Daniel Metwater, I never saw him as the type to hurt a kid."

"I think he's a sociopath who's capable of anything," Ethan said.

He found Michelle slumped against his cruiser, arms folded over her chest, head down. She straightened at his approach. "Well?"

"Asteria says Metwater couldn't open your trunk, so he gave it to two guys named Eugene and Derek and told them to get rid of it. Do you know them?"

"Eugene is the guy who found that bloody sock," she said. "Derek is just a bully. The two of them are loyal to Metwater because he lets them throw their weight around. That's the only kind of men who stay with him for long— that, and a few hangers-on who are hoping for a chance with all the women he attracts."

"Why did Hunter's father leave?" He couldn't imagine walking out on the mother of his child, or leaving his son without a father.

He held the passenger door of the cruiser open for her. "I know you said he wasn't interested in being a father, but did something specific happen to make him quit the Family?"

"He thought I was obsessed with the Prophet." She slid into the passenger seat and reached for the seat belt. "I couldn't tell him the real reason I wanted to be here—about Cass and David Metwater and everything. He was too much of a talker. I knew if I told him he wouldn't be able to keep the information to himself." She shrugged. "He hated living out here, and he was too immature to be a father. I couldn't depend on him."

"You and Hunter deserve someone you can depend on."

"It's okay. I'm used to looking after myself."

He turned toward her, the anger he had been suppressing too long, surfacing. "I get that you're capable of looking after yourself, but you shouldn't have to. You should have people in your life you can depend on to be there for you."

"Yeah, well, I should be able to eat ice cream three times a day without gaining weight, too. The world isn't perfect. I'd think a cop would know that."

"I know it." He started the cruiser and shifted into Reverse. "But I don't have to like it."

He backed out of the parking lot and headed down the rutted forest service road, following the rooster tail of dust raised by Carmen's vehicle. Michelle remained silent, though he could feel her gaze on him. "What I don't like is how men like David and Daniel Metwater get away with anything," she said. "And no one listens to the people they hurt, like me."

"I'm listening," Ethan said.

"Yeah, you are. But I thought you'd be able to do more. Why don't you arrest him?"

"It doesn't do any good to arrest someone if you don't have the proof you need to keep him in jail," Ethan said. "We don't have anything that links Metwater to your son's disappearance."

"He stole my trunk. Isn't that enough to lock him up, at least for a little while?"

"He's saying you abandoned the trunk, and that it was his property anyway because of the agreement everyone signs when they join the Family."

"I didn't sign the agreement." She gripped the dashboard as they bounced over a washboarded section of road. "And I didn't abandon the trunk."

"We'll keep looking for it, but you might want to start trying to get copies of the important papers that were in it—birth certificates, that sort of thing."

"You don't think I'll ever see the things that were in there again."

"I'm saying it's possible they're gone for good."

She fell silent again. He scanned the landscape of sagebrush and juniper, wishing he could find the right words to give her something positive to hang on to. Her son had been missing over twenty-four hours now. Every hour that passed lessened the chances they would find Hunter alive. The idea made him angry all over again.

"Is that smoke over there?" Michelle said. She pointed out the front windshield. He leaned forward and squinted at the thin gray column rising up from the ground. A simple campfire wouldn't make that much smoke, unless it had gotten out of control. Wildfire was a constant concern here in the high desert. One errant cigarette butt or abandoned campfire could lead to the destruction of thousands of acres of public land.

He shifted into Low and turned the cruiser off the road and began bumping his way toward the column of smoke. Michelle leaned forward in the seat, straining to see ahead of them.

Ethan braked the cruiser well back from the blaze. The fire had consumed an area about four feet square. Whoever had set it hadn't tried to be subtle. Ethan could smell the gasoline as he climbed out of the driver's seat. He pulled a fire extinguisher from the back of the vehicle, then started toward the blaze, Michelle on his heels.

He pulled the pin on the extinguisher and sent a cloud of suppressant over the smoldering ground at the perimeter of the main blaze. Michelle broke a green branch from a nearby piñon and began beating the ground with it, extinguishing sparks as she moved forward.

Ethan hit the center of the blaze with the full force of the extinguisher, engulfing the flames and coating everything in white. When he could no longer see flames, he took the branch from Michelle and used the end to tease apart the smoldering logs to reveal a blackened shape beneath.

Michelle gasped. "It's my trunk," she said.

She would have reached for it, but Ethan held her back. "It's too hot to touch," he said. And everything in it was likely ruined—the top had caved in and fire had all but consumed most of one end. "We'll get a crime scene team out here to investigate," he said. "They'll save whatever they can of the contents."

"He wants to destroy me." She stared at the smoldering trunk, eyes unfocused, the words so soft Ethan wasn't even sure she realized she had said them.

He touched her arm, lightly, the way he would approach a sleepwalker. She glanced at him, no recognition in her gaze. "He wants to destroy me, the way his brother destroyed Cass," she said. "But I won't let him. I won't." Then she turned and walked back to the cruiser, leaving Ethan standing on the blackened ground.

Chapter Nine

Ethan drove Michelle back to Ranger Headquarters, and then he and a crime scene team
returned to the smoldering remains of the
trunk. The team photographed the area, took
measurements and hauled the trunk away
for processing. "You've done all you can for
today," Commander Ellison said when Ethan
reported back to headquarters. "Take Michelle
back to the duplex and both of you try to get
some rest. The helicopter we asked for got di-
verted to the Front Range, but we've resched-
uled the air search for tomorrow."

"Will do." Ethan walked over to where Michelle sat slumped at a desk, a cold cup of coffee at her elbow. "Ready to get out of here?"
he asked.

She nodded. She didn't say anything until
they turned onto the highway from the park

road. "Nights are the worst," she said. "I'm exhausted, but every time I close my eyes I think about Hunter, alone somewhere in the dark." She bit her lip, and he could feel the force of her willing herself not to cry.

"I think we're all really good at torturing ourselves with thoughts like that," he said. "For weeks after my dad died I couldn't sleep for wondering if I could have done something to save him. He had a heart attack while he was painting the back fence. I told myself I should have painted the fence for him, or persuaded him to hire someone to do the job." He shook his head. "Useless to think all that, but I couldn't stop myself."

Michelle angled toward him. "When did he die?"

"Six months ago." He tightened his grip on the steering wheel. "It's one of the reasons I took the job with the Ranger Brigade. My mom lives in Montrose and I wanted to be close to her."

"That's really nice," she said. "And I'm sorry about your dad. But if his heart was bad, even if you had painted that fence, wouldn't the problem have shown up some other time?"

Ethan nodded. "Of course it would have. And the truth is, my dad liked painting things.

He died doing something he enjoyed, and I guess we can't ask for better than that."

"I'll bet he was a really nice guy," she said. "Because you're a nice guy. I never knew my father. I'm not sure my mom even knew who he was. The one thing I really beat myself up about is being too much like my mom that way—I should have been more careful, and waited to give Hunter a real dad."

"Lots of kids these days don't have two parents and they do okay," Ethan said.

"Yeah, but I can't help thinking a boy needs a good man in his life."

Ethan's dad had been a good man—the best. He glanced at Michelle. "Would you mind if we ran by to see my mom for a few minutes?" he asked. "I like to check on her a few times a week. My dad was the kind of guy who did everything for her, and I think she's having a tough time now that he's gone."

"Sure," she said. "I'd love to meet her."

The first thing Ethan noted when he pulled into the driveway at his mother's house was that the yard had been mowed and trimmed. Nancy Reynolds came out onto the front stoop as Ethan and Michelle stepped out of the car. "Mom, this is Michelle Munson." He made the introduction as his mom walked out to meet them. "Michelle, this is my mom, Nancy."

"You're that poor mother whose little boy is missing, aren't you?" His mom took Michelle's hand in both of hers, her face creased with concern. "I saw the reports on the news. I've been praying they find him."

"Thank you," Michelle said. "Your son has been a big help to me."

Nancy nodded. "He is a big help to me, too."

"Mom, who did the yard?" Ethan asked.

"Althea Douglas gave me the name of the people she uses and they came out this afternoon." She surveyed the yard. "I think they did a pretty good job. They'll come every week now."

"Mom, I told you I would take care of it."

"You have plenty to do without worrying about my yard." She pulled Michelle toward the house. "Come on. I've got a surprise to show you."

Ethan followed the two women. His mom pressed the button to open the garage door and it slowly rose to reveal a shiny blue sedan with dealer tags. "It's the first brand-new car I've ever owned," she said, excitement making her voice sound high and girlish. She turned to Michelle. "Ethan's father always bought used cars. Which is very practical, I'm sure. But I always wanted something new." She leaned over and patted the fender of the car, an Accord.

Ethan fought a storm of emotions, from worry to anger. "Mom, why didn't you say something to me?" he asked. "I would have gone with you."

"I wanted to do this for myself," she said. "It was important to me to do it on my own."

"I hope they didn't take advantage of you," he said. His inexperienced mother would have been a target for an unscrupulous salesman.

"I didn't accept the first price he quoted," she said. "I made him come down, and I did my research online so I knew what was fair."

"It's beautiful," Michelle said. "And I love the color."

"Let me take you for a drive," his mom said. "She rides like a dream. Just let me get my purse." Before Ethan could protest, she ran back into the house.

"I can't believe she just went out and bought a new car," Ethan said, staring after her. "What was she thinking?"

"She always wanted a new car," Michelle said. "Why shouldn't she have it?"

Ethan didn't have an answer to this question. It wasn't the new car he minded, so much as his mother's impulsive—and as far as he was concerned, uncharacteristic—behavior. Maybe this was the first sign of early dementia. Today she was buying a new car—tomorrow she might donate her savings to a fake charity.

She emerged from the house, holding up the key fob. "I don't even need an old-fashioned key," she said. "Can you believe it?" She climbed into the driver's seat.

"You sit up front with your mom," Michelle said as she opened the back door.

Ethan slid into the front passenger seat. "Leather seats," Michelle said. She ran an appreciative hand over the upholstery. "Nice."

"Kenny—that was my husband, Ethan's father—didn't like leather seats. Impractical, he called them."

"But you didn't want practical," Michelle said. "You wanted good-looking. Luxurious, even."

"Exactly!" His mom beamed and backed the car out of the garage. "And right now I want to treat the two of you to dinner," she said.

"That's okay, Mom," Ethan said. "You don't have—"

"All three of us have to eat," his mom said.

"So hush, and let me buy it for you." She raised her voice to be better heard in the back seat. "Ethan never wants me to spend money. I keep telling him that his father left me well provided for, but he doesn't believe it."

"You have to be careful, Mom," he said. "Dad took care of all the finances, so you haven't had a lot of experience with all that."

"Believe it or not, I still know how to add and subtract," she said. "And I know how to handle money. You don't have to worry about me winding up penniless on your doorstep."

"It's really sweet of you to offer to buy dinner," Michelle said. "But going to a restaurant where the press might see us isn't a good idea."

"Then I know the perfect place," his mom said. "Trust me, the press will never find you there."

Which was how the three of them ended up at Dixie's Drive-in. The old-fashioned drive-in on the outskirts of town boasted killer onion rings, real ice cream shakes and fresh-ground burgers on toasted buns. "We used to come here almost every Saturday night when Ethan was young," his mom said after they had placed their orders.

"This was always where Dad took me when he wanted to have a serious talk," Ethan said.

"We'd order burgers and rings and after the food came Dad would make whatever announcement he wanted me to hear and we would eat. I think he liked that the food kept us from having to say too much more once he was done with his speech."

"What kind of announcements?" Michelle asked.

"This is where he told me about sex when I was eleven years old." Ethan chuckled, remembering. "He had a whole speech about the physical realities of sex and he recited it in a monotone, and very fast. His face was as red as the bottles of ketchup. I let him get through the whole thing before I told him my best friend, Mark Greeley, had already told me everything and that I had already French-kissed Carol Sue Beemer behind her father's barn when I went over to help harvest corn."

"Shame on you," his mom said. "Your poor father agonized over having 'the talk' with you for weeks. I finally told him he had to get it over with before he drove me crazy."

Ethan settled back in his seat. The car smelled so new—not like any vehicle the family had ever owned. "We talked about other things, too," he said. "About grades and sports, where I wanted to go to college, what I wanted to do for a living."

"He was always so proud of you," his mother said. "'My son, the FBI agent,' he would say."

"He always told me he hoped I found a woman like you," Ethan said.

His mom dabbed at her eyes. "For goodness' sake, I hope you find a woman better than me." She gave a watery smile. "Someone who knows how to balance her own checkbook and isn't terrified of spiders."

"Fearlessness is overrated," Michelle said. "Ethan likes taking care of people, so he needs a woman who needs to be looked after."

"We all need looking after sometimes, don't we?" his mom said. "I think sometimes the toughest people need that most of all."

MICHELLE ACHED FOR her son. She dreamed she was standing by that fire in the wilderness, walking through the ashes, opening the blackened trunk. Hunter, her beautiful boy, smiled up for her. But when she bent to lift him up, she discovered it was only a doll that looked like Hunter—plastic and staring and not her boy at all.

She woke crying, Ethan holding her tightly against him. She pressed her face into his chest, breathing in the clean cotton scent of the T-shirt he wore, and the more elemental fragrance of his skin, warm and male, comforting and exciting even in the midst of her grief.

She clung to him, yet hated that she did so. You couldn't hold on to people. If you tried, you only ended up hurt. If you counted on others for help, you'd only end up weaker than ever. Better to fight your own battles. Better to not need anyone else.

But when his arms tightened around her and he murmured soothing words in her ear, she could only hold on more. She had always been strong, but this time she wasn't strong enough to let go.

Last night, after dinner with his mom and the drive back to the duplex, fatigue had dragged at her. She didn't ask Ethan to stay with her, but when he did, she had been beyond relieved. She didn't think she would have slept at all if she had had to spend the night alone.

After a while she was able to pull herself together and ease out of his arms. "What time is it?" she asked.

"Almost seven," he said. "I have to be at work at eight. Do you want to grab a shower while I fix breakfast?"

She pushed her hair out of her eyes. "A shower would be good. But I don't feel like eating."

"I don't imagine you do, but it will probably be a long day." He stood and began pulling on clothes. "You need to eat something."

She shuffled into the shower, trying to decide how she felt about this—about him taking care of her—fixing breakfast and telling her to eat. She was a grown woman. She didn't need someone telling her what to do.

She still couldn't believe she had said that last night, about Ethan needing someone to look after. It was probably true, but was that really something you should say to a man's mother? All she had really meant to do was to subtly point out that she was not the woman for Ethan—just in case his mom started getting ideas.

Not that she didn't like Ethan—she was crazy about him. He was probably the best man she had ever met. But she had worked hard for many years to be someone who could always look after herself, and Ethan was never going to really appreciate that.

She couldn't imagine being like his mother—having to rely on other people for everything from mowing the lawn to handling her checkbook. Props to her for getting out there and learning new things, but it sounded as if she still had a ways to go. It had been a long time since Michelle had had a checking account, but she still knew how to take care of one. She knew how to change a tire and pick a lock and how to work her way through the paperwork maze of social services. She knew what she had to do to take care of herself and Hunter.

Hunter. Maybe they would find him today. Surely they would. Last night Ethan had explained they were bringing in a helicopter to search the area for any signs of the little boy. And volunteers from town were going to do a grid search of the wilderness around the camp. There was still the possibility that he had wandered off on his own and was lost somewhere in all that empty land. She shuddered at the thought. But children that young could survive amazing things, couldn't they? She had read stories like that—toddlers wandering lost for days, drinking ditch water and eating wild berries, eventually found safe and sound. That could happen for Hunter, too.

But her gut told her her son hadn't wandered off on his own. Someone had taken him— Daniel Metwater or someone Metwater controlled.

Ethan had coffee and scrambled eggs and

toast waiting in the kitchen. "Should I go with the volunteers to search this morning?" she asked as he set a plate in front of her.

"You can, though it might be better if you stay at headquarters, in case we get any news." He took the seat across from her and began slathering strawberry jam on a piece of toast. "We've got another group of volunteers that will be putting up fliers all over the area. Someone might remember seeing Hunter."

"Why are people doing this?" she asked. "All these volunteers, I mean? They don't even know me."

"People care," he said. "Especially when a child is involved. They want to do what they can to help."

A knock on the door startled them. Ethan set down his toast and rose, frowning. He left the room and she heard the door open and muffled voices. A moment later Ethan returned. "It's a reporter from the *Montrose Daily Press*," he said. "He wants to speak to you."

Her stomach knotted. "I don't want to talk to anyone."

"You don't have to," Ethan said. "I'll send him away."

When he left the room again, she followed,

trying to stay out of sight behind him. "She doesn't want to talk to you," Ethan said.

"Just a few words and a picture," the reporter said. "It will help the volunteers to see who they're helping."

The thought of all those people helping her when she didn't even know them nagged at her. She stepped forward. "All right. But just a few words."

"Great." The reporter, a stocky young man with thinning blond hair, beckoned her forward. "Step out here where the light is better."

She moved onto the front steps of the duplex, and was startled to see half a dozen reporters congregating there. Camera flashes momentarily blinded her and for a moment she was sixteen again, standing in front of her foster parents' home, surrounded by an angry crowd who thought she had killed a little girl.

Only Ethan's hand pressed against her lower back kept her from fleeing back inside. She cleared her throat. "I want to thank everyone for their help," she said.

"Tell us about your son," the reporter prompted.

"Hunter…" Her voice broke and she struggled to control it. She didn't want to break down, though that was probably what some of them wanted. People liked drama. "Hunter is a good little boy," she said. "Always cheerful and loving. He's fearless, too. He loves meeting new people. If you find him—when you find him—you'll see."

"Do you think your son's disappearance has any connection to the disappearance of Madeline Perry, a child who was also under your care ten years ago?"

Her shock over the question must have shown on her face. The cameras flashed again, and she put up a hand to protect her eyes. Ethan moved up beside her, his hand still at her back. "Before you go making accusations, you'd better get your facts straight," he said, his voice full of anger. "Madeline Perry was kidnapped by her mother, who had lost a custody dispute with the child's father. Ms. Munson had nothing to do with the disappearance."

"That's not what my source said," the reporter said.

"Who is your source?" Ethan asked.

The reporter smirked. "You know I can't reveal that."

"Your source is wrong."

He ushered her inside and closed the door and locked it. She leaned against the wall, shaken. "Daniel Metwater fed the reporter that information," she said. "He's doing everything he can to get at me."

He led her back into the kitchen and sat her at the table, then refilled both their coffee cups. "Why is Metwater after you?" he asked.

"I don't know. Maybe because of his brother—because of what I know about David."

"Were they so close he would hurt you to keep you quiet?"

"They were twins. People say twins have a special bond."

"Or maybe he was involved somehow in David's crimes and he doesn't want that to come out." Since their first conversation along these lines he had tried to figure out some connection between the two brothers that would lead to his harassment of Michelle, but he had come up with nothing.

"I'm not going to let him beat me." She pushed away the half-eaten breakfast. "I'm tougher than he thinks."

"I'm not going to let him beat you," he said. "And if he's responsible for what you and Hunter have suffered so far, I'll make sure he pays."

The fierceness of his words made her throat tighten. She couldn't believe all cops took their jobs so seriously—there was something very special about Ethan Reynolds.

Breakfast done, Ethan fended off the reporters who crowded around as they made their way to his cruiser. Michelle half expected to see a similar horde outside Ranger Headquarters, but either the press hadn't made their way here yet, or the Rangers had warned them off.

Inside, they found Carmen and Simon examining the contents of the burned trunk, which were spread on tables in the conference room. Everything reeked of smoke and most of the items were unrecognizable, reduced to twisted shards of black.

"They used diesel fuel as an accelerant," Simon said. "We found some tire tracks in the area, but nothing we can link to a specific vehicle."

Michelle stopped in front of what was left of her photo album. She started to reach for it, then stopped and looked at Ethan. "May I?"

"Sure."

She slid the blackened book toward her and gingerly lifted the cover. Relief flooded her when she saw the first page. "The edges are a little scorched, but I think most of the pictures are okay." She flipped through the pages, stopping on her high school graduation photo.

She looked so impossibly young at first glance, though anyone who studied her eyes might see some of all she had been through by that age.

"Is that you?" Ethan asked.

She nodded. "I like the picture, so I kept it."

She turned the page to a group of snapshots of Hunter—as a newborn in the hospital, then slightly older, in the bath, smiling his wonderful smile. She blinked back tears and closed the book. "I can't accept that he just vanished," she said.

Ethan pulled another book from farther down the table. "Are these the articles you saved about David Metwater?" he asked.

She forced her attention to the scrapbook in front of him. "Yes. I started collecting them after Cass's death." The scrapbook hadn't fared as well as the photo album in the fire—many of the pages were scorched to the point where they were unreadable.

"We can probably find most of this stuff on-line." Simon joined them. "If we reassemble the collection, maybe we can pinpoint something in there Metwater is worried about."

"If you have a computer I could use, I could start looking," she said. That would give her something to do, and something to focus on while she waited on word from the searchers.

"You can use my laptop," Carmen said. "We'll set you up with a desk. Send anything interesting you find to the printer."

She hadn't used a computer in months. A couple of times since joining up with Metwater, she had looked up things on the desktop units at the local library—mostly checking for any updates on Cass's or David Metwater's deaths.

An internet search for the names Daniel Metwater and David Metwater pulled up a number of articles, some familiar, some new to her. A small article in an alternative Chicago paper caught her eye. Entitled "The Making of a Prophet," it detailed Daniel Metwater's transformation from industrialist to evangelist. "Metwater says the death of his twin affected him deeply and made him see the futility of his materialistic way of life. He longed for peace and found it in a retreat to the wilderness. Afterward, he felt called to teach others the lessons he had learned.

"However, our search revealed the Prophet did not divest himself of his worldly goods. In fact, his fortune has increased since he began leading his group of followers in the Colorado wilderness. One requirement of joining the group is that members contribute their possessions to the Family—of which Metwater is head. His latest coup is the recruitment of prominent socialite Andi Matheson. Daughter of the late Senator Pete Matheson, Andi has a personal fortune estimated at several million dollars. Much of that money is tied up in trusts that will revert to her—and presumably to Metwater—when she turns thirty later this year."

Michelle printed off this article. She wondered if Asteria would be so favored after she turned thirty and signed over all her millions to Daniel Metwater.

She scrolled through more articles, reading about the brothers' inheritance of their father's manufacturing millions, about David's murder and rumors of embezzlement from the family firm and ties to the Russian Mafia. Daniel Metwater presented himself as the squeaky-clean son, the good twin who had only tried to help his brother and now grieved his passing.

She found a couple of articles about Cass—only one mentioned that the hotel room she was found in after she died had been rented to David Metwater. After a few days her name disappeared from the news altogether, forgotten by all but those, like Michelle, who had loved her.

She was so absorbed in her research, she failed to notice anything going on around her. Only when Ethan stopped by her desk did she look up, blinking. "Something's come up," he said, and the grim expression on his face made her heart pound.

She half rose from the chair, then sank down again, too wobbly to stand. "What is it?" she asked. "Have they found Hunter? Is he—?"

"We haven't found him." He gripped her shoulder, his eyes locked to hers. "As far as we know, he's all right. But we've received a note."

"A note?" She looked around, confused.

Simon joined them and handed her a single sheet of paper, encased in a plastic envelope. "This came in the mail a few minutes ago. Postmarked in Montrose, addressed to you, in care of this office."

She blinked, bringing the block letters typed on the paper into focus:

WE HAVE YOUR KID. WE WANT ONE MILLION DOLLARS FOR HIS SAFE RETURN. TELL YOUR RICH FRIENDS TO PAY UP OR YOU'LL NEVER SEE HIM AGAIN.

Chapter Ten

Ethan took the note from Michelle. Her hand trembled and all the color had drained from her face. "Is this a ransom note?" she asked. "For a million dollars?" She shook her head. "Why would anyone think I have that kind of money?"

"Who are these rich friends the note mentions?" Simon asked.

"I don't have any rich friends," she said.

"What about Andi Matheson?" Simon asked. "Asteria. You and she shared a tent at Metwater's camp."

"Yes, but—I never thought of her as rich."

"She is," Simon said. "Though most of the money is in a trust, she still has access to some of it."

"Or Metwater does," Ethan said. "Don't his followers sign over their money to him?"

"Then maybe Metwater is the rich friend they're referring to."

"Who sent this?" Michelle asked.

"That's what we're trying to find out." Simon took the letter from Ethan. "Do you have any ideas?"

She shook her head. "No. It's crazy."

Simon tapped the evidence envelope against his palm. "Metwater seems pretty money-motivated to me," he said. "Maybe this is a ploy to get at some of Asteria's money outside of the funds that are tied up in her trust."

"I don't know why he would need to do that," Michelle said. "She would give him anything he wanted."

"Are you sure about that?" Ethan asked. "If she knows he's cheating on her, maybe withholding money would be a way for her to get back at him."

"Or maybe he thinks she could break the trust for something like this," Simon said. "I think we should bring him in for questioning."

"You're going to bring him here?" Michelle asked. "He won't like that."

"Good," Ethan said. "I want to make him as uncomfortable as possible."

"And while he's here, we'll send a team out to the camp again," Simon said. "Maybe without Metwater around, his followers will be more likely to answer our questions honestly."

"I guess getting this ransom note is a good thing, right?" she asked. "It means Hunter is still alive, and not wandering alone in the wilderness—or worse."

The yearning in her expression tore at Ethan. He wanted to lie to her, to tell her that yes, that was the case. But kidnappers were just as likely to ask for ransom for someone who was already dead. Or some people might try to make money by capitalizing on something they had only heard about on the news. He didn't want to raise Michelle's hopes, only to have them dashed later. "We don't know," he said. "I hope so, but we can't be sure."

She nodded. "The note didn't say anything about how I'm supposed to get in touch with the kidnappers, or how to get the money to them—if I could come up with such a crazy sum."

"They'll probably follow up with another note or a phone call," Simon said. "We'll be ready when that happens. We'll try to trace the call. A letter will be tougher, but we'll do what we can to try to track down the sender."

"What do I tell them when they get in touch?"

"We'll give you a script to follow," Ethan

said. "And we'll be right there with you. You don't have to deal with this on your own."

She nodded, but he had the sense she didn't really believe him. Hunter was her child—this was her private pain. He couldn't ease her suffering or take that burden from her, though each day he knew her he wanted to do that more and more.

She was a tough, prickly person who seemed to go out of her way to keep others at a distance, but he had glimpsed the sweetness she carried deep inside her. He wanted to find a way to show her that it was safe to let that side of her show more—to let other people into her life.

To let him in.

ETHAN AND SIMON, with Marco Cruz and Michael Dance as backup, drove to Metwater's camp at the base of Mystic Mesa to bring him in for questioning. "You know he's going to put up a fight," Simon said as he pulled his cruiser into the parking area for the camp.

"I hope he does," Ethan said. "I'd like an excuse to give him a little taste of what he dealt to Michelle."

"I hear you." Simon checked his Glock, then slid it back into the holster at his hip. "I'm not so concerned about Metwater—I think he's mostly talk and a coward. Guys that target women and children usually are. But he keeps a bunch of young muscle around him. They're the ones we need to watch out for."

"We can handle them." Marco tapped the stun gun on his belt.

Ethan glanced up the path toward camp. "My guess is he knows we're here by now. He'll have had lookouts."

"Let's go," Simon said, and led the way up the path.

The compound looked deserted, all the trailers and tents shut tight, an eerie silence hanging over the clearing. A breeze stirred a child's beach ball in front of one trailer, and laundry flapped on a line hung between two trees, but the camp looked abandoned. "Do you think Metwater orders them to hide when the cops show up, or is it just their guilty consciences at work?" Simon asked, looking around.

"They're watching us," Ethan said. He walked up to the door of the motor home and knocked. No answer. Michael and Marco moved around to the back of the RV, just in case Metwater decided to duck out a window. Ethan knocked again. "Open up, Metwater," he called. "We need to talk to you."

The door opened, faster than Ethan had expected. He had his gun drawn before Metwater stepped out. Metwater scowled. "Are you planning to shoot me?"

Ethan eased the gun back into the holster and struggled to control his breathing. "We need you to come with us to Ranger Brigade Headquarters," he said.

"No." Metwater folded his arms across his chest and scowled.

"You don't even know why we want you there," Simon said.

"It doesn't matter. I'm not going."

"We weren't making a suggestion." Simon took hold of Metwater's arm, but the Prophet shook him off.

A muscular young man stepped out of the motor home behind Metwater. He didn't say anything but stood next to the Prophet, muscles flexed.

"Don't even think of trying anything," Simon said. He unclipped the stun gun from his belt and reached for Metwater's arm again. "Don't make this harder than it has to be."

"Don't touch me!" Metwater jerked back and spat the words, his face flushed with rage. "You have no right." The muscle lunged for Simon and the Ranger fired the stun gun, the prongs catching the young man in the shoulder. He groaned and staggered back, then fell backward into the motor home.

Metwater stared at his bodyguard, who was writhing on the floor as Simon knelt beside him.

"We need you to come to headquarters and answer a few questions," Ethan said. "Cooperate and you could be back in time for dinner."

"And if I don't cooperate?"

"Then we'll charge you with impeding a police investigation and take you into custody," Ethan said.

"I don't have time to go with you now," Metwater said. "I'm preparing for an important presentation I'm giving in Omaha next week."

"You won't be going anywhere next week if you don't cooperate," Simon said. He had removed the stun gun leads from the young man and left him in the care of a young woman, who had emerged from the back of the motor home, possibly from the bedroom.

"Where's Asteria?" Ethan asked.

"She isn't here." Metwater glanced at the young woman. She looked up at him with a worshipful expression that made Ethan a little queasy.

"Where is she?" Simon asked, menace in his voice.

"I sent her away for a while. All this turmoil wasn't good for her."

"Where did you send her?" Simon moved closer, crowding Metwater up against the doorjamb.

"That's none of your business."

Simon's body tensed. Ethan was sure his fellow officer was going to deck Metwater—or hit him with the reloaded stun gun. He stepped between them. "People seem to have a way of disappearing from your camp lately," Ethan said. "First Hunter Munson, now Andi Matheson. You need to tell us where she is."

Metwater pressed his lips together and remained silent.

Simon turned to the young woman, who still knelt on the floor beside the young man, who was sitting up now, and glaring at the two officers. "Where is Asteria?" Simon asked.

"I... I don't know," the young woman said. "She and the Prophet left this morning. She took a suitcase with her. He returned a couple of hours ago."

"Did she go willingly?" Simon asked. "Was she upset or afraid?"

"She seemed okay to me," the young woman

said. "It's hard to tell with her, though. She's not the warm and friendly type."

"What did they leave in?" Ethan asked. "Did someone drive them?"

"The Prophet drove." The young man spoke, with the nasal, clipped tones of the upper Midwest. "He used that old beater Starfall used to drive."

"We'll get a team in to search the car," Simon said, his gaze fixed on Metwater. "If we find anything suspicious, all the lawyers in Colorado won't be able to help you."

Ethan took hold of Metwater's arm. The man tried to resist, but Ethan held tight. Simon took hold of his other arm, pulled it behind him and snapped on the cuffs. "Am I under arrest?" Metwater asked.

"You're a person of interest," Ethan said. "We need you to answer some questions about the disappearance of Hunter Munson and Andi Matheson."

"Asteria hasn't disappeared. She's perfectly safe. And I already told you I don't know anything about Hunter."

"We've had a new development in the case," Ethan said. "We need your input."

"I don't have to talk to you. I want my lawyer."

"You can call him from headquarters." Ethan nudged him forward, toward the steps.

Marco and Michael rejoined them in front of the motor home. "Question anyone you can find in camp," Simon said. "See if any of them know where Andi Matheson went this morning."

"She's resting and doesn't want to be disturbed," Metwater said.

"Tell us where she is and you'll save yourself a lot of trouble," Ethan said.

"You're the ones who are going to be in trouble once I get hold of my lawyer," Metwater said.

Ethan tugged him toward the cars. "I'm more worried about Ms. Matheson than I am about your lawyers," he said.

Metwater clammed up then, and Ethan tucked him in the back of the cruiser. Neither he nor Simon spoke on the long ride back to Ranger Headquarters, though Ethan sensed his partner's agitation. They had left Michael and Marco to deal with the other residents of camp, and to wait for the crime scene team to search Michelle's car. He only hoped they would turn up something positive.

At Ranger Headquarters, they led Metwater into the conference room. "I want to call my lawyer," he said as Simon uncuffed him.

"Fine. Tell him you're a person of interest in the disappearances of Hunter Munson and of Andi Metwater," Ethan said. "And tell him we want to know why you sent a ransom note for a million dollars to Hunter's mother."

He had hoped to catch Metwater off guard with the accusation, but the Prophet's response was not at all what he expected. Metwater dropped into a chair, his face pale. "A ransom note? What are you talking about?"

"Show him," Ethan said.

Simon retrieved the evidence envelope and held it up in front of Metwater. "Look familiar?"

Metwater scanned the note, his expression growing more agitated by the second. He jumped up from the chair. "Those idiots!" he shouted, and tried to push past Ethan.

Ethan didn't think; he reacted. He landed a punch that dropped Metwater to his knees, and the Prophet toppled to the floor, out cold.

Chapter Eleven

Michelle hated being stuck in this back office with a computer, unable to hear or see what was going on elsewhere in Ranger Headquarters. But Ethan had stressed that she couldn't be involved in questioning Daniel Metwater, and it would be better for everyone if he didn't even know she was here.

She guessed she could understand that—but that didn't mean she didn't want to keep tabs on what both Metwater and the Rangers were up to. Yes, Ethan and the other Rangers had been great with her so far, but they were still cops, and she didn't trust them to put her interests first. Only she could do that.

So when she heard the hum of conversation in the front room rise, she crept to the door of the office where they had put her and peeked out. Sure enough, Daniel Metwater stood in the middle of the room, surrounded by Rangers. The angry, arrogant expression on his face made her stomach churn. She wanted to launch herself at him and demand he tell her what he had done with her son—to kick and scratch and destroy him the way he was trying to destroy her.

Ethan took Metwater's arm and led him toward the conference room. Only then did she see that the Prophet's hands were handcuffed behind him, and giddy relief staggered her. She clung to the doorjamb while relief surged through her. If they had Metwater in cuffs, that must mean they had arrested him. Had they found some proof linking him to Hunter's disappearance? Would she be reunited with her son soon?

She forced herself to remain quiet and hidden as Ethan and Simon led Metwater into the conference room and shut the door. She had to give them time to question him—to make him tell them what he had done with Hunter.

Eyes closed, forehead pressed against the smooth wood of the door, she tried to picture the reunion with her son. He would smile his beautiful smile and reach out his chubby little arms for her. She would hold him and rock him and breathe deeply of his sweet scent, and reassure him that he was safe.

The door to the conference room opened and Simon emerged. He retrieved something from his desk, then went back in. A few seconds passed, and then a loud shout from the conference room made her jump. Sounds of a struggle, a loud smack, then a thump that shook the floor beneath her feet.

She came out of the office. Lance Carpenter ran past her. "What's going on?" she asked. He didn't answer but kept going, so she followed. She burst into the room in time to see Metwater facedown on the floor, Ethan kneeling in the middle of his back, cuffing him. "What happened?" she asked.

Ethan looked up at her. "You aren't supposed to be here," he said.

"But I am. So tell me what happened."

"We showed Metwater the ransom note and he went ballistic," Simon said.

Ethan rose and pulled Metwater to his feet. "Want to tell us what that was about?" he asked. "Who are the idiots you were referring to?"

"I want to talk to my lawyer."

"Fine." Ethan pushed Metwater toward the

door. "Lance, call Montrose lockup and tell them we're bringing in a prisoner."

"You can't arrest me," Metwater protested. "I haven't done anything."

"We'll start with assault on a police officer and go from there," Ethan said. "Simon, take him for me. I'll catch up in a minute."

Simon took hold of Metwater, and Ethan crossed the room to Michelle. "You come with me," he said.

She folded her arms over her chest and took a step back. "What if I don't want to?"

His expression softened. "Please?"

"All right." She followed him back to the office where she had been waiting before.

He closed the door behind them and faced her. "Did you find anything else interesting online?" he asked.

"I printed out a few more articles, but none of them had any new information."

"We'll have a couple of people take a look at them—maybe we'll spot something."

"What happened with Metwater?" she asked. "I saw you brought him in in handcuffs—did you arrest him? Did you find something to link him to Hunter? Did he tell you where Hunter is?"

He put a hand on her shoulder. "We don't

know anything more about Hunter," he said. "I'm sorry."

She struggled not to let her disappointment show. "Then tell me what's going on."

"Andi Matheson—Asteria—has disappeared."

She definitely hadn't been expecting that. She gaped at him. "What?"

"She left camp this morning with Metwater—in your car. He returned a few hours later without her. He admits that much, but he won't say where she is—only that she went away to rest."

She swallowed hard. "I can't believe he would hurt Asteria. Not that he cares about anyone but himself, but she was worth a lot of money to him."

"Do you know if she had a will? It's possible she left everything to him, in which case she might be worth more to him dead than alive."

She shook her head. "I don't know. But I don't think so. She never said anything about it. Wouldn't she have to see a lawyer for something like that? She never mentioned it." She hugged herself, trying to ward off the chill that engulfed her. Asteria had been her one friend in the camp, and she was so close to having her baby.

"It's possible Metwater is telling the truth and is just being a jerk by not telling us where she's hiding," Ethan said. "Do you know where she might have gone? Did she mention a favorite place, or a friend or relative she might turn to?"

"No. She always said she had no one—that the Prophet and his followers were her only family now. She said she never wanted to go back to her old life."

"We've alerted area law enforcement to be on the lookout for her, and we'll contact area hotels in case he stashed her in one of them. And we'll lean on him to reveal her whereabouts, though his lawyers will try to prevent us talking to him."

"Simon said he went crazy when he saw the ransom note," she said. "What was that about?"

Ethan stepped back. "We don't know. He shouted 'those idiots' and lunged at me."

"It sounds like he knows whoever wrote the note."

"Yeah. It sounded like that to me, too." He grasped the doorknob. "I have to go now, and I'm not sure when I'll be back. If you want to get out of here, you can ask someone to take you back to the duplex."

"I want to stay here, in case some news comes in about Hunter," she said. "I just wish there was something more I could do."

"I know it's hard," he said. "But you need to hang on and let us take care of this. We're doing everything we can."

She nodded and he left. She sagged into the desk chair. She wanted to believe that he would *take care of this*, but wasn't that the polite thing that people said? In the end, Hunter was her child. She was the one who suffered most from his disappearance. And when this was all settled, one way or another, she was the one who would have to deal with the outcome. Ethan and the others would go on with their lives and she would have to find a way to go on with hers. Alone. That was the way things always ended up for her. She couldn't let herself believe that would change now, just because she'd met a cop who showed more compassion than most, and he was a man who touched parts of her no one else had ever been able to reach.

METWATER'S LAWYER WAS waiting for him when he arrived with Ethan and Simon at the Montrose County Jail. "What are the charges against my client?" the attorney, a stocky man with a full head of silver hair and a reputation as a legal bulldog, demanded as soon as the two Rangers marched Metwater into the building.

"Assaulting an officer, and interfering with the investigation of a crime, for starters," Ethan said. "He's also a suspect in the disappearances of Hunter Munson and Andi Matheson, aka Asteria."

"Defending oneself against police brutality is not assault," the lawyer shot back. "Refusing to answer questions without an attorney present is not interfering with an investigation, and you don't have as scrap of evidence to tie him to the disappearance of either of those people."

"Amazing," Simon said. "You know all this before you've even spoken with your client."

"I'm familiar with how you people operate." The lawyer glanced at Metwater, whose stony expression hadn't changed. "I want a conference room and the opportunity to speak with my client in private."

"You can do that," Ethan said, "after we process him."

Even as he filled out paperwork, then led Metwater downstairs to be photographed and fingerprinted, Ethan held out little hope that Metwater would stay in jail for long. He had money and influence, and the best they could expect was to keep him a few hours before he posted bail.

He was surprised, therefore, when only a few moments after Metwater was led into an interview room to meet with his attorney, the Prophet sent word that he was ready to speak with Ethan and Simon.

"My client is prepared to make you an offer," the attorney announced when Ethan and Simon were seated across the table from Metwater and his counsel.

"How generous," Simon said. "What makes him think we're interested?"

"Mr. Metwater is prepared to tell you where Asteria is staying, in exchange for you dropping all charges against him. Charges, I might add, which will never hold up in court."

"If they won't hold up in court, why does he want to deal at all?" Ethan asked.

"He would like to avoid the hassle of a trial and return to his home. His followers need him."

"His followers need him like they need hemorrhoids," Simon muttered.

Ethan cleared his throat. "Your client needs to tell us what he knows about the disappearance of Hunter Munson."

"There's nothing to tell," the lawyer said. "He doesn't know anything."

"When we showed him the ransom note we received, he said something about idiots—and then he exploded," Ethan said.

"You must have misunderstood him. He doesn't know anything."

Metwater sat with his arms folded, expressionless, a silent, brooding figure more statue than man. Ethan glanced at Simon. "We need to talk about this."

The lawyer gestured toward the door. "By all means."

In the hallway, Simon paced. "We've got him cold on the assault charges," he said. "We've got video of him trying to hit you."

"And what will that get him?" Ethan asked. "A slap on the wrist. Everything else we've got is weak. Meanwhile, Andi Matheson could be the key to this case."

"How do you figure that?" Simon asked.

"I don't think going away was her idea. I think Metwater sent her away so that we couldn't get to her. She knows something about Hunter's disappearance. She's eight months pregnant and Hunter is a missing baby—no matter how loyal she is to Metwater, that's got to be preying on her mind. She's going to tell us what she knows."

"Maybe if we talk to her, we can persuade her not to go back to Metwater's camp," Simon said. "She needs to see what a creep he is."

"Right, but we need to talk to her. And we can't do that if we don't know where she is. Given time, we might find her on our own, but depending on where Hunter is, we might not have the time."

Simon stopped pacing, shoulders slumped. "So we take Metwater's deal."

"We take the deal, and gamble that whatever Andi gives us will be enough to nail him with a bigger charge later," Ethan said. "We've still got the assault on Michelle we can hold over his head. I think I could persuade her to press charges now."

"Why wouldn't she press charges when it first happened?" Simon asked.

"She has a bad history with the police. They took her through the wringer when that little girl she was babysitting disappeared." It still angered him when he thought about her going through that, so young and so alone. "It didn't help that Metwater was making so much noise about her being responsible for her son's disappearance. She thought we would believe him."

"I don't believe anything he says." Simon glanced toward the closed door to the interview room. "How do we know he won't just tell us a lie this time? What if we let him go and find out Andi isn't where he says she is?"

"Then we pick him up again," Ethan said. "That will be part of the deal—he can't leave town until our investigation is over. We'll have someone watch the camp to make sure he stays put."

"The commander will love that idea—not."

"But he'll agree, because he knows how important this is."

Simon nodded. "Let's do it, then."

Metwater and his lawyer broke off their conversation when the two Rangers returned to the room. "Well?" the lawyer asked.

Ethan ignored him and addressed Metwater. "You tell us where Andi Matheson is and if she's there, we drop the assault charge and the charge of interfering with our investigation."

"She's at the Brown Palace in Denver," Metwater said. "I took her to the airport this morning, and arranged for a car to pick her up and deliver her to the hotel. She hated to leave me, but I persuaded her it would be best for her and her baby to get out of this tense situation for a while."

The lawyer stood. "I believe we're done here."

"You can go," Simon said to Metwater. "But we'll be keeping an eye on you. And we had better not find out you lied to us."

In the hallway once more, Ethan looked up the telephone number for the Brown Palace Hotel and Spa. "Pretty fancy retreat," Simon said. "You ever been there?"

Ethan shook his head.

"It's one of the oldest hotels in Denver— very Victorian and luxurious. Lots of presidents and famous people have stayed there. Metwater might have made a mistake, putting her there."

"How do you figure that?" Ethan asked.

"It will remind her of her old life as a rich socialite," Simon said. "A few nights of sleeping on expensive sheets and having spa treatments and she might not want to come back to the wilderness."

Ethan transmitted the number and listened to it ring. On the third ring a pleasant woman's voice answered, "The Brown Palace Hotel and Spa. How may I help you?"

"This is Special Agent Ethan Reynolds with the FBI. Do you have an Andi Matheson registered there?"

"One moment please, Agent Reynolds."

Ethan waited, and a moment later a man came on the line. "This is the general manager, Roger Able," he said. "How may I help you?"

"I'm looking for a woman named Andi Matheson. She hasn't done anything wrong. I'm merely trying to determine that she's safe."

"Our guest information is confidential. How do I know you're who you say you are?"

"I'll give you a number you can call to verify my credentials." He rattled off the number and Able promised to call it, then call him back. Ethan ended the call.

"We should have held Metwater in custody until we had this all settled," Simon said.

"We know where to find him," Ethan said. "And Michael is following him."

His cell phone rang and he answered it. "Agent Reynolds, I've checked our registration, and we don't have an Andi Matheson registered here," Able said. "We don't have anyone named Matheson."

"How about Asteria? Or Metwater?"

"One moment please."

Simon's scowl deepened. "We should have asked Metwater what name she was registered under."

Able came back on the line. "I'm sorry, but we don't have anyone by those names, either."

Ethan bit back a groan of frustration. "We're looking for a blonde young woman, very pregnant, who checked into the hotel this morning," he said.

"I don't know of anyone here who fits that description," Able said. "But I only came on this afternoon."

"Then I think the best thing is for you to send me a list of all your registered guests."

"I can't supply that information without a warrant."

It was the answer Ethan had expected, but he had to try. "I'll be in touch," he said, and ended the call.

"I'll go to the hotel in Denver," Simon said. "If she's there, I'll find her."

"That's probably the best way to make sure she's really safe," Ethan said.

"I'll clear it with the commander," Simon said, and pulled out his phone.

While Simon talked to Commander Ellison, Ethan called Michelle. "You must be exhausted," he said. "It's going to be a while before I'm free. Let me take you back to the duplex while I have a few moments free and you can try to get some rest."

"All right. Your side or mine?"

Was it a good sign that she was asking the

question? "Wherever you feel more comfortable," he said. "You're welcome to stay in my side."

"All right." He wasn't sure how to interpret that—was she going to stay in his side of the duplex or hers? He guessed he'd find out when he got home—whenever that ended up being.

"Have you heard anything from the volunteers who are looking for Hunter?" she asked.

"I'm sorry, no."

"I watched a local news broadcast and they showed his picture. Maybe someone will see him and recognize him." She sounded so down—clinging to this frail hope with her last strength.

"I hope so." He wanted to be able to give her good news, but right now the only positive in this whole case was that they hadn't found Ethan's body. "Hang in there," he said. "I'll be home as soon as I can."

"I'll be okay." But the words held no conviction.

Simon approached as Ethan stowed his phone. "I've got the okay to go to Denver to find Andi," he said. "I'll drop you back at headquarters, then head over to my place to clean up and pack."

"All right." Ethan planned to spend some

time going over the printouts Michelle had compiled about Metwater. Maybe he would see something there that would give him a clue to the man's thought processes, why he was targeting Michelle and what his next move might be.

Activity was winding down at headquarters when Ethan arrived. The commander and a few others had gone home, though they would be in early in the morning to start another round of searching for Hunter Munson. Michelle looked drained, dark half-moons beneath her eyes and skin so pale it was almost translucent. "Is there anything you need before I take you back to my place?" he asked. "Anything you want to eat or drink—ice cream?"

She tried to smile but didn't quite make it. "Thanks, but I don't need anything from a store."

No—all she needed was the one thing he couldn't give her—her son. "What are you going to be doing this evening?" she asked as they climbed into his cruiser.

"I'm going to do some more digging into Daniel and David Metwater's backgrounds," he said. "I'm hoping I'll spot something that will tell me why you have him so worried. If

I can figure out his motive, maybe I'll have a better handle on what he's done with Hunter."

"So you really do believe Metwater took Hunter," she said.

"I believe he probably had something to do with Hunter's disappearance, yes." He glanced at her. "That doesn't mean I'm not keeping my mind open to other possible suspects."

"I overheard people talking today," she said. "Rangers and volunteers and others— and some of them still think Hunter wandered away on his own."

"At this point we can't risk ruling out anything or anyone," he said. "We don't want to look in the wrong direction and miss the one clue that will lead us to finding him."

"I know, but—"

His phone rang, shrill and insistent. He glanced at the dash screen that showed an incoming call and sighed. "What is it?" she asked.

"My mom." He tapped the button to ignore the call.

"Why aren't you going to answer it?" Michelle asked.

"She probably just wants to talk, and I don't have time for that right now."

"I don't mind if you pull over and talk to

her," Michelle said. "It's not as if I'm in a big hurry to get to the duplex and spend more time waiting."

"It's not that." He shook his head. "Sometimes I don't know what to say to her. When she talks about Dad, it makes me sad. When she asks me things like what color she should paint the living room, I have no idea. I mean, what's wrong with the color it is now? And things she should ask me about—like that new car—she doesn't say a word."

"Wow—you really are wound up about that car, aren't you?"

He risked another glance at her. She was regarding him calmly, some of the fatigue gone from her eyes. "You think I'm making too big a deal of it, don't you?" he asked.

"I think you're a good son who misses his father and wants to take care of his mother," she said. "And like most men, you think your job is to fix things. Your mom doesn't need that."

"Then what does she need?"

"You could ask her. But you might try not offering an opinion or advice at all. Just listen. When she talks about your father, maybe share some of your own good memories of him. It might help you, too. Tell her whatever color she paints the living room is fine by you. And tell her you're proud of her for handling the car purchase by herself. It's a big deal, and she's proud of herself for doing it, so you should be, too."

The phone rang again. This time, he answered, Michelle's advice—which he wasn't sure he agreed with—spinning in his head. "Oh, Ethan, I'm so glad I was able to reach you." His mother sounded breathless—a little teary, even.

Ethan pulled the cruiser to the side of the road. "What's wrong, Mom?" he asked. "What's happened?"

"My car! Someone stole my new car!" Her voice rose to a wail on the last words.

Chapter Twelve

"Calm down, Mom. Take a deep breath and tell me exactly what happened." Ethan tried to sound calm, to handle his mother the way he would a distraught witness.

"I went to have my nails done—you know I have that done every other week," she said. "All the spaces in front of the salon were full, so I had to park at the end of the lot by the street. When I came out, the car was gone."

"Are you sure?" Ethan asked. "It's a new car, so you're not used to it. Maybe you parked in a different spot than you remembered."

"Ethan Reynolds, I know where I parked my own car."

He winced at her tone of voice—the same one she had used when she learned he had been caught cheating on a history test in eighth grade, and when he had gotten his first speeding ticket at age seventeen. "Did you call the police?" he asked.

"Yes. And they took a report over the phone, but the officer didn't sound like he took me seriously. So now I'm calling you. You're FBI—you ought to be able to find my car."

"I'll do what I can, Mom. I promise." He wrote down the description of the car and the name of the officer who had the theft report, and promised to call her when he knew more, then hung up and pulled back onto the road.

"Your poor mother," Michelle said after a moment. "She must be beside herself."

"She was pretty upset." He tapped his fingers on the steering wheel. "The local cops won't appreciate a fed homing in on their case."

"They'll understand when you explain the car belonged to your mother," Michelle said. "Besides, can't you tell them it's Ranger business? You handle car thefts, don't you?"

The image of a collection of license plates spread out on the conference room table flashed into his head. "We do," he said. "Do you remember the night Simon and I came to Metwater's camp—the night he beat you?"

"I'm not going to forget that night—ever."

"We were there to question him about a car theft ring we think was operating near the camp. We thought maybe one or more of his followers might be involved. Did you ever hear anything about that—Family members getting money from stolen cars or car parts or anything like that?"

"Nothing like that, exactly. We have a guy, Roscoe, who was sort of our family mechanic. He worked on my car a few times and he kept a lot of other folks' rides running. But he also made money selling junked cars he finds out there. I guess people haul wrecks out there and dump them sometimes."

"Or maybe they aren't all wrecks," Ethan said. "Maybe some of them used to be new cars."

"I don't think so," Michelle said. "I mean, he didn't only sell junk cars. He sold old appliances and stock tanks and anything else he found abandoned. The stuff I saw him with was always old and beat up and rusty."

"Still, I think I'll have a talk with him," Ethan said.

"I hope you find your mom's car," she said.

"If an organized gang like this one stole it, it's already been cut into pieces or is on its way out of state," Ethan said. "Probably the best I can do is help her file the insurance claim and pick out a new one."

"Ask her if she wants help with the papers," Michelle said. "Let her pick out her own car."

"Right." He grimaced. He still had a lot to learn about handling women, including his mother.

ETHAN DROPPED MICHELLE off at the duplex, then headed to Ranger Headquarters. She prowled the rooms, unable to rest despite her exhaustion. She distracted herself by examining Ethan's belongings, trying to imagine the life he lived here. He wasn't overly neat, or a slob, the kind of man who valued utility over appearance. The kitchen contained the basics, but nothing extra—no mixer or juicer or anything extraneous. His bookshelf contained law enforcement texts, nature guides and some historical novels. The only picture on his wall was a painting of an elk bugling, against a backdrop of snowcapped peaks.

His furniture was identical to the items in the other half of the unit, which meant it had probably been here when he moved in. The one exception was a sturdy but worn leather recliner, positioned for watching the flat-screen television. She settled into this chair, and it was almost as if Ethan had wrapped his arms around her. The leather carried his scent. She imagined him sitting here, feet up, remote in hand, as he flipped through channels, looking for a game. He had probably spent many such evenings for the chair to conform to the shape of his body this way.

She hadn't bothered asking him if he had a girlfriend or if he dated. He struck her as something of a loner—lonely, even. Though she had spent much of her life on her own, she rarely thought of herself as lonely. Though now she was so grateful not to have to endure the pain of waiting and wondering about her son without Ethan to steady her.

She was almost asleep when her cell phone buzzed. She shifted to dig it out of her pocket and frowned at a number she didn't recognize, then sat bolt upright, heart racing. What if it was the kidnappers? She didn't have the script Ethan had promised. She had no way of tracing the call.

The ringtone continued, insistent. With shaking hands, she swiped to answer it. "Hello?"

"Hello, Starfall? It's me, Asteria."

"Asteria?" It took half a second for the name to register; then a second surge of adrenaline jolted her. "Where are you? Everyone's so worried about you."

"You don't need to worry about me," Asteria said. "I'm fine. The Prophet sent me to a spa to rest. I didn't really want to go, but he convinced me it would be the best thing for the baby."

"Where did he send you?" Michelle asked.

"I'm in Denver. And I'm fine, really. Have you had any word about Hunter?"

"Nothing yet."

"Oh, no. I was hoping they would have found him by now."

"They haven't." The pain of this truth stabbed her all over again. "Asteria—Andi—do you know anything at all about what happened to him? I know you wouldn't have had any part in taking him, but maybe Metwater said something or did something—"

"He didn't. I even asked him directly if he knew anything about Hunter's disappearance."

"What did he say?" Not that she expected he would tell the truth, but his answer might be revealing.

"That's one reason I called," Asteria said. "I wanted you to know that the Prophet had a vision. He said in the vision he saw Hunter safe and happy. He's fine and you don't need to worry."

Michelle gripped the phone so tightly her fingers ached. "The only way he could know that was if he had something to do with Hunter's kidnapping," she said.

"No!" Asteria protested. "The Prophet has a true gift. His visions are real."

"His visions are a way of manipulating his followers," Michelle said. "Andi, wake up!" She deliberately used the woman's real name, to remind her of who she really was. "Don't let him manipulate you, too."

"I called because I thought you'd be happy to hear some good news," Andi said. "Instead, you tell me I'm stupid."

"I don't think you're stupid," Michelle said. "But you're being naive if you think everything Daniel Metwater tells you is true."

"He's the only one who has ever accepted the real me." She sounded teary now. "You're the kind of person who always sees the worst in people, instead of all the good they do."

Michelle couldn't deny the charge. For much of her life, that had been true. But lately, she'd felt something shifting inside her. "I see the good in you," she said. "And I care about you—and about your baby. Just promise me that if you have any doubts—or you're ever in trouble and need help—you'll go to the Ranger Brigade. They care, too, and they'll help you."

"I can't believe you, of all people, are recommending I rely on the police for anything," Andi said.

"I can't believe it, either," Michelle said. "But it's true. They've done everything they can to help me, and I know they would help you, too."

"I don't need their help. I don't need anyone's help. And I'd better go now. I'm sorry I called."

"I'm not sorry," Michelle said. "It was good to hear from you, and I'm glad to know you're all right. But please, think about something. If Daniel Metwater did have something to do with Hunter's disappearance—if he would take a child from his mother—what would he do with your baby?"

"I can't believe you'd say something so awful," Andi said, and ended the call.

No, Michelle thought. *You just don't want to believe your Prophet would do something so awful*.

ETHAN PORED OVER the computer printouts about the Metwater brothers until his head ached and his vision blurred, but he could find nothing to link Daniel to his brother's crimes or to anything else he might have needed to keep Michelle from revealing.

At last, he put the files aside and drove home. The light was on in the front room, and when he unlocked the door and stepped inside, he was surprised to find Michelle asleep in the recliner, an afghan his mother had knitted draped over her. At least someone was getting some rest. He was tempted to leave her there, but as he passed the chair, she stirred.

"What time is it?" she asked, blinking and wincing at the light.

"It's after midnight. I'm sorry I woke you."

"It's okay." She pushed aside the afghan and stretched. "Your chair is really comfortable," she said.

"It was my dad's." That and a hunting rifle were the only two things he had wanted of his father's. As far back as he could remember, the leather recliner had been his dad's throne, the place where he read the paper, watched the ball game and meted out both punishment and advice to his only child.

"It's yours now," she said, rubbing one hand up and down the arm of the chair. "It smells like you."

He didn't know what to say to that, and decided instead to answer the question she hadn't yet asked. "I didn't find anything in the files," he said.

"I didn't really think you would, but thanks for trying." She yawned and sat up straighter. "Before I forget, Asteria called. She said she's safe and staying at some spa in Denver."

"Metwater told us she was at the Brown Palace, but it's nice to have that confirmed. Is that why she called—to let you know where she was?"

Michelle shook her head. "She said something else that she thought I'd be happy to hear, but it only made me angrier."

He sat on the sofa adjacent to the recliner, only inches away from her. "What was that?"

"She asked Metwater if he knew anything about Hunter's disappearance. He told her he had had a vision. In the vision he saw Hunter, safe and happy. I tried to tell her that if Metwater knew that Hunter was safe, it meant he had something to do with him being taken from me—either that, or he's lying to make her stop worrying."

"But she doesn't see it that way," Ethan said.

"No. She thinks he's really a prophet and his visions are real. I told her she shouldn't trust him, but of course she didn't listen. She said I always thought the worst of people." She clasped her hands, her fingers laced. "The thing is, she's right. I have always looked for the worst in everyone."

"From what you've told me, you've had good reason not to trust people," Ethan said.

"Maybe. But I'm trying to change." Her eyes met his, weary but focused. "I told her if she ever needed help, she should contact the Rangers. I told her she could trust you—that I trusted you."

He leaned over and took her hand and held it. "I'm glad I've earned your trust," he said. "I'll do everything in my power to keep it."

She leaned forward and kissed him, then closed her eyes and rested her head on his shoulder. "What happens now?" she asked.

"Now? We're both exhausted. I think we should go to bed."

"All right."

He stood and pulled her up beside him. Then, leaning on each other, they walked to his bedroom and helped each other undress. They climbed under the covers and she snuggled close. He thought she might have been asleep before he turned off the light. That, he realized, was proof of how comfortable she had become with him.

It took longer for him to go to sleep, his

mind too full of everything that had happened—with Michelle and Hunter and his mother and Metwater. Tomorrow he would need to follow up on the theft of his mother's car, and maybe find time to go by Metwater's camp to question Roscoe. He might have another go at Metwater, also—ask him about the *vision* he had described to Asteria. It seemed he had scarcely drifted off before his phone rang. He groped for it on the bedside table and answered groggily.

"Ethan, it's Carmen. Did I wake you?"

"What time is it?" He squinted at the bedside clock.

"It's almost eight."

He swore under his breath and swung his feet to the floor. "I'll be in as soon as I can," he said. "I had a late night last night."

"I'm not calling to rag on you for being late," Carmen said. "I wanted to let you know we just had someone call in with a report of two young men and a baby staying at an old motel in Cimarron. The caller thought that was odd. It may be nothing, but we should check it out."

"I'm on it." He pulled a pad of paper and a pen from the bedside table. "Give me the address."

Carmen read off the address. "Simon is already on his way."

"I thought he went to Denver."

"He had car trouble last night and got such a late start he decided to wait until this morning. He wasn't likely to get anything out of the folks at the Brown Palace in the middle of the night."

"Tell him I'll meet him in Cimarron," Ethan said.

"You and half the force," Carmen said. "None of us want to be left out of this one."

He ended the call and turned to find Michelle sitting up in bed, staring at him. "What is it?" she asked.

"We got a report of two guys with a baby— it could be Hunter."

She threw back the covers and headed toward her clothes. "Wait," he said. "It also might be nothing. Don't get your hopes up."

"Hope is all I've got," she said. "I'm coming with you."

"You can't."

"Why not? I'm his mother."

"I promise you, if it is Hunter, as soon as it's safe to do so, you can see him," Ethan said. "But I can't let you walk into a potential hostage situation. Having you there might even make the kidnappers less likely to cooperate."

She continued dressing. "I'm going with you."

He walked around the bed and took her shoulders. "Michelle, look at me."

She glared at him. "He's my baby. He needs me. I need him."

"Yes, but I need you to stay safe while we make sure he's safe, too. Do you remember you said you trusted me?"

"Yes. Because I thought you were on my side."

"I am on your side. And I need to keep both you and Hunter safe." He gave her a gentle squeeze. "I promise, I will bring you to him, as soon as it's safe to do so. But I can't do my best for him if I'm worried about you, too."

"Then don't worry about me," she said. "The only person you need to worry about is Hunter."

He cupped her cheek in his palm. "I can't avoid worrying about you. That's how important you've become to me."

The hardness went out of her eyes. She wet her lips. "All right. I'll stay here. But save my boy. Bring him back to me."

"If this baby is Hunter, I'll get him back

to you." He had taken an oath that he would give his life, if necessary, to protect and serve, but he had never meant the words more than he did now.

Chapter Thirteen

In the cruiser, Ethan called Carmen again. "Give me an update."

"Colorado State Patrol is already headed that way to sit on the place and make sure these guys don't leave until we've checked them out. The rest of us are mobilizing. Where is Michelle?"

"I left her at my place. She wasn't happy about it, but I tried to make her understand it wouldn't be safe for her or Hunter to have her there."

"Ouch. That's tough."

"You're telling me. I promised her as soon as it was safe to do so, I'd bring her to him."

"You did the right thing."

"Yeah. But I'm not sure she believed that." He slowed as he neared the small community of Cimarron, which boasted one gas station, a post office and a few campgrounds and motels mainly utilized by fishermen and people visiting Blue Mesa Reservoir or Black Canyon of the Gunnison National Park. "I'm almost at the motel," he said. "I'll do a drive-by and see what I can see."

The Magpie Inn consisted of a row of seven connected rooms, all facing the highway, a big picture window in each room giving a clear view of the road and the parking lot. The office sat to one side of the rooms. Anyone in the rooms or the office would spot a police vehicle as soon as it drove in, so Ethan sped past. If anyone at the motel saw him, he hoped they would think he was on his way somewhere else.

Just beyond the inn, a silver and blue Colorado State Patrol unit had parked on the side of the highway. Ethan swung his cruiser in to park behind it. A uniformed deputy stepped out of the patrol car to greet him. "Mike Gladwell," he said, shaking hands.

"Ethan Reynolds." Ethan nodded toward the motel. "Can you tell me anything about this place?"

"The owner is an older couple, the Johansons," Gladwell said. "The wife is the only one there right now. I talked to her on the phone when the call first came in. She says the two guys registered as brothers—Thad and Tom Smith. The baby is Thad's son, Timmy. They're in room six—next to the last on the end farthest from the office."

"I suppose that could be their real names," Ethan said.

"I ran the plates on the car," Gladwell said. "It's a rental—rented to Thad Smith. They rented a car seat along with the car."

"Who called this in, do you know?" Ethan asked.

"The motel owner, Mrs. Johanson, thinks it's the wife of a couple in the room next to the Smiths, on the end. The lady was asking the owner about these guys—she said it didn't look to her as if they had a clue how to take care of a baby."

"Anything else we should know?" Ethan asked.

"Mrs. Johanson said they haven't acted like your typical vacationers. No sightseeing or hiking or fishing or anything. They've pretty much stayed in the cabin, out of sight."

"Where is the owner now?" Ethan asked.

"I talked her into locking up and going to her house up there." Gladwell pointed up the hill from the motel. "She'll stay there until I give her the all clear, and she promised to call her husband and let him know not to stop by here. He planned to spend the morning fishing."

Two other Ranger cruisers pulled in behind Ethan's vehicle and Carmen, Lance and Simon got out. After introductions, Lance asked. "What's the plan?"

"Someone needs to watch the back while Simon and I approach the front," Ethan said.

Simon nodded. "We'll park behind the office," he said. "Where they can't see us. Then we'll approach their door from the side, on foot."

"We'll take the back," Carmen said.

"I'll watch the parking lot exit," Gladwell said.

"All right," Lance said. "Let's do it."

They checked their weapons, then took their positions. Simon pulled his cruiser in behind the office and he and Ethan stayed close to the building, out of sight of anyone in the rooms. They moved quickly, weapons drawn. When they reached the room the Smiths were registered in, they positioned themselves on either side of the door and Ethan knocked.

No one answered, but the curtains over the window twitched. Ethan knocked again, harder. "Mr. Smith, we need to speak with you, please."

The door opened, and a man in his twenties with shaggy brown hair and the bronzed skin of someone who spent a lot of time out of doors peered out. He wore a faded blue T-shirt and tan cargo shorts and was barefoot. "What's going on?" he asked.

"Child welfare check," Ethan said. "Do you have an infant here with you?"

"Uh…"

Ethan figured he was about to lie, but at that moment a baby began to wail, somewhere in the room behind the young man. He glanced over his shoulder. "That's just my son, Timmy."

"May we see him, please?"

"Why?"

"A woman called in a concern about his welfare."

Thad—if that was really his name—swore under his breath.

"We need to make sure the child is all right," Simon said. "If you could just bring him to the door for a moment."

"Uh, sure." He stepped back and shut the door. The sounds of movement and low, muffled voices followed.

Ethan's eyes met Simon's across the door. "What do you think?" he asked.

"I think if he doesn't come out of there in thirty seconds, we go in," Simon said.

The gun blast tore through the door, sending wood splinters flying. Both officers flattened themselves on the ground. Ethan began scooting backward, away from the room, his eyes on the door. Though he held his weapon at the ready, he didn't dare fire blindly into the room, for fear of hitting Hunter.

"Let us go and the kid won't get hurt," Thad called. "Try anything and he's dead, I swear it!"

MICHELLE HAD TO muster every reserve of strength to keep from racing down the driveway after Ethan as his cruiser pulled away. While objectively, his words about keeping clear and staying safe, letting the Rangers do their job, all made sense, her mother's instinct to be with her child and protect him threatened to overwhelm any practical logic. Hunter needed her. He was probably frightened and confused right now, and she was the only one who could comfort him.

She forced herself to stand and go into the kitchen. She'd make coffee, and then maybe find something to watch on television. She would do her best to distract herself, all the while waiting for the call that would tell her her son was safe.

She was pouring coffee into her cup when a knock on the door startled her so much she almost dropped the carafe. She froze and the knock came again, louder this time. Was it another reporter, wanting to badger her with questions? Or someone from the Rangers with news about Hunter?

Heart pounding, she crept across the floor to the door and peered out the security peephole. She choked back a cry of alarm when she found herself staring into Daniel Metwater's intense dark eyes. He pounded the door again. "I know you're in there, Michelle." He sneered her name. "Open up so we can talk."

Her first instinct was to remain silent and refuse to answer, but even as she was pondering this, he backed up and gave the door a vicious kick. It shook in its frame. A second kick had it buckling inward near the doorknob. She looked around wildly for something—anything—with which to defend herself, and spotted the phone. If she called, could Ethan or one of the others get to her in time?

She had just reached the phone when the

door burst open and Metwater rushed in, smashing his way toward the kitchen. Her coffee cup shattered as he grabbed hold of her arm and wrenched the phone away. He hurled it to the floor and stomped on it, bits of plastic flying as he crushed it. She stared at him, unable to speak. Gone was the mild-mannered, charismatic Prophet, replaced by a fierce, angry bully. He dragged her across the room and shoved her onto the sofa. "You're going to sit there and you're going to listen to me," he ordered.

Be tough, she told herself. *Don't let him see how scared you are.* She sat up straight and forced herself to look him in the eye. "Whatever you have to say, you'd better say it quick. Ethan will be home any minute. When he finds you here he'll have you back in jail so fast you won't know what hit you."

"Your boyfriend isn't going to bother us," Metwater said. "He and that other cop, Woolridge, were headed in the opposite direction last time I saw them."

"How did you find me?" she asked.

"I followed you from Ranger Headquarters last night."

"You're supposed to be in jail."

"They had to drop the charges," he said. "I

knew they would. They didn't have a scrap of proof that I was guilty of anything but being someone they don't like. Everybody knows the Rangers like to harass me and my followers."

"Asteria called and told me what you said about Hunter—that you knew where he was. That's proof you had something to do with his disappearance."

"It doesn't prove anything. I'm a prophet, remember? I have visions and I know things." He moved toward her. "The way I know that you're not going to cause me any more trouble."

She jumped up and tried to run away, but he grabbed her arm and yanked her back onto the sofa. "You're not going anywhere," he said. He kneeled over her, pushing her back into the cushions.

She forced herself to keep looking at him, trying to read his intentions in his eyes, but all she saw in his expression was the mania of a fanatic, and a hatred that chilled her to the core. "I hate liars," he said, his hands on her arms tightening so that she bit back a cry of pain. "You've been lying to me ever since we met—pretending you wanted to follow me when all you really wanted was to bring me down."

"I don't care about you," she said. "I only wanted to know the truth about your brother, David."

He laughed, throwing his head back, his body shaking with mirth. "You want to know the truth? You wouldn't believe it if I told you."

"Your brother killed my sister," she said. "He gave her those drugs and let everyone think she had overdosed."

"No, he didn't do that." He shook his head. "I don't expect you to believe me, but my brother didn't do any of the things people think he did. But he'll never have the chance to clear his name. Isn't that ironic? He and your sister—your foster sister—have that in common."

"Did you know Cass?" she asked. "Did you ever meet her?"

"Yes, I did. She was a lovely young woman. And a very stupid one. If she had kept her mouth shut, she might still be alive. But she had to say the wrong thing to the wrong person. Just like you." He squeezed harder, and she whimpered. She tried to fight him, but it was like pushing against a wall. Where was Ethan? If only he would come back with Hunter in time to save her.

Metwater straightened and pulled her up alongside him. "Come on," he said.

"Wh…where are we going?"

"Out." He dragged her toward the door.

"I'm not going anywhere with you." She tried to pull free, but he shook her and slapped her, hard, blurring her vision.

"Shut up!" He yanked open the door and pulled her outside. She blinked at the familiar car in the driveway. Her car.

She opened her mouth to speak and tasted blood. Icy terror gripped her so that her vision blurred and it hurt to breathe. She couldn't go with him. If she did, she would never come back alive, she was sure. She dug in her heels and hung back.

"Stop it!" He yanked her forward with one hand while he pulled the keys from his pocket with the other.

She looked around wildly—for a weapon, for someone who could help her, for anything she could use to get away. But there was nothing. The other duplexes on this short dead-end street were all home to other members of the Ranger Brigade, who were all away, trying to rescue her son. No traffic passed on the road that connected to the street, and the neat, sparse yard offered nothing she could use as a weapon.

Metwater opened the passenger door and

dragged her toward the car. She made herself go limp, her heels digging into the dirt, resisting him with all her strength. He grunted and took hold of her with both hands. "Let me go!" she shouted, and kicked at him, ignoring the pain that shot through her as he wrenched her shoulders. She managed to free one hand and clawed at his face, her nails raking across his skin.

Enraged, he let out a roar and grabbed hold of her hair, yanking her head so far back she thought he might break her neck. She spit at him and writhed in his arms. If she pulled him to the ground, maybe she could crawl away from him...

"No!" he shouted, and slammed her against the side of the car. Pain exploded in her head, and a flash of bright light blinded her, right before darkness engulfed her and that riptide she had been fighting earlier pulled her completely under.

Chapter Fourteen

Ethan crawled backward along the walkway in front of the row of hotel rooms until he reached the corner of the building and cover. He pulled himself to his feet and looked back in time to see Simon disappear around the opposite corner of the building. They were both safe, but what about the men and the baby in that room?

His telephone buzzed and he answered it. "We heard the shots," Carmen said, her voice just above a whisper. "What's going on up there?"

"They fired on us," he said. "They've got Hunter in there and they said they'll kill him if we try anything."

"Who are they?" she asked. "Why did they take Hunter?"

"No idea. Did we ever track down Michelle's ex?"

"No. We weren't able to find him."

"Maybe he's one of these guys." Ethan wiped the sweat from his forehead. "It doesn't matter. We have to figure out how to get Hunter out of there before things go south."

"We need to get a hostage negotiator out here," she said. "Maybe we can talk them into giving up the baby."

"I've had training as a hostage negotiator," Ethan said. "I'm going to call the commander and see what he wants to do."

"Okay. Simon is with us now. He seems okay."

"Good. We don't want anyone hurt if we can help it." He hung up and punched in Commander Graham Ellison's number. The commander answered on the first ring.

"What's going on out there?" Ellison asked. "A report came in on the scanner of shots fired."

"We've got two guys, registered as Thad and Tom Smith, with a baby we're pretty sure is Hunter Munson," Ethan said. "Simon and I went to the door of their room and asked to see the baby. I spoke to Thad, who pretended to cooperate, then opened fire and screamed if we tried anything, he'd kill the kid."

"You okay?" Ellison asked.

"I'm safe. So is Simon. He's behind the building with Carmen and Lance. We've got a CSP deputy posted at the road. Before we got here he persuaded the motel owner to move to her house nearby, so she's out of the line of fire."

"Don't do anything until I get there with reinforcements," Ellison said. "Keep quiet and let them sweat a little."

"Will do." He ended the call just as Simon slipped up beside him from behind the building. "You okay?" Ethan asked.

"Yeah." He nodded toward the kidnappers' room. "What's the plan?"

"The commander and the rest of the team are on their way. We're to sit tight until they get here."

"Is anyone staying in any of these other rooms?" Simon asked.

Ethan had been so focused on Hunter and the kidnappers, he hadn't even thought about other people who might be in harm's way. "I'll find out," he said. "Gladwell knows the owners. He can tell us how to get in touch with them."

Keeping out of view of the kidnappers, he

slipped behind the office and made his way to the road. A second Colorado State Patrol car had parked behind Gladwell's. Both CSP deputies walked back to the rear of the second car to meet Ethan. "Everybody okay?" Gladwell asked.

"So far," Ethan said. "We're waiting for our commander and some more of the team to get here. Do you know if there are other guests staying here?"

"I asked Mrs. Johanson and she says she had three other rooms rented, but their occupants are all out sightseeing or fishing or other stuff," Gladwell said. "I'll give you her number and you can double-check. I know she'd appreciate an update about what's going on. We'll keep any other guests away if they come back before this is resolved."

"Thanks."

"What's the game plan?" Gladwell asked.

"My commander is on his way," Ethan said. "We'll try talking first, see if we can get them to hand over the kid."

"We can get a sniper over from CSP if you need one," the second deputy said.

"Thanks," Ethan said. "We've got that covered, I think." Marco Cruz had that kind of experience. They'd position him where he had a clear view of the door and window of the room, though the Smith brothers had the curtains pulled over the latter. Still, if they stepped out the door, Marco might have to chance a shot. Ethan had been on a hostage situation once where, after more than twelve hours of negotiating for the release of two children, he persuaded the kidnapper to accept a delivery of pizza. As soon as he stepped onto his front porch to pick up the boxes, the sharpshooter nailed him. It wasn't the ideal outcome, but they had saved the two kids.

Ethan would do whatever it took to save Michelle's kid. Hunter deserved a chance to grow up. And Michelle deserved to see her son again.

Ethan rejoined Simon. "Gladwell says all the other guests are out. I'm going to call the owner, Mrs. Johanson, to double-check and to find out more about the layout of the rooms." He punched in the number Gladwell had given him.

"Johanson," a man answered, his voice gruff.

Ethan identified himself and brought the man up-to-date on what was going on with the Smiths. "I wanted to know more about the layout of the rooms," he said. "Is there a door connecting the room the Smiths are in to the rooms on the other side?"

"There is," Mr. Johanson said. "It should be locked and bolted from the other side, though."

"What about windows?" Ethan asked. "Anything large enough for a man to crawl out of?"

"There's a small window in the bathroom at the back," Johanson said. "But it's only about eighteen inches wide. I don't think either of the Smiths could fit through it."

"Okay. Does the room have a phone?"

"All our rooms have phones and satellite TV. People expect that these days."

"I'll need the number for the phone in their room. We're going to try to negotiate with these guys."

"I feel terrible about that kid," Johanson said. "I guess we should have realized something wasn't right, but we don't watch much news and we're just not the type to expect the worst from people. Let me get you that number."

He came back on the line after a moment and rattled off the phone number, which Ethan wrote down in his notebook. "Is there anything we can do?" Mr. Johanson asked.

"Just stay in the house. We'll let you know when it's safe to come out."

"Here comes the cavalry," Simon said as Ethan pocketed his phone. Two Ranger Brigade FJ Cruisers swung in to block the entrance to the motel, and Commander Ellison and the rest of the Ranger Brigade climbed out. Simon and Ethan made their way over to meet them.

Ethan brought them up to date on the situation, opening his notebook to sketch the layout of the rooms. "We could put a team in the room next door and come in that way," Marco said.

"Risky unless we know exactly where the baby is," Commander Ellison said.

"I might be able to find that out when I talk to them," Ethan said.

"The back window is a little small to try going in that way," Ellison said.

"Carmen might be able to get in that way," Simon said.

"I wouldn't want to send her in alone," Ellison said. "But we'll keep it in mind."

"We come at them from both sides, it'll be easier to pin them down," Simon said.

Ethan shook his head. "Too much risk of the baby getting caught in the cross fire."

"Ethan, you get them on the phone," Ellison said. "Maybe we can talk them into surrendering. Meanwhile, Simon and Michael, you get into the room next door. We'll keep Carmen and Lance on the back of the building, and tell her to be ready to go in the window if necessary. Marco, you take up a position where you have a clear shot at the front of the room."

WHAT IS THAT roaring in my ears? And why is it so dark?

Michelle groaned, and the roaring faded, her vision gradually clearing. Her head throbbed, and her arms ached. What was she doing lying in the back of a car? She struggled to sit, the task made more difficult by the fact that her hands were tied behind her back.

"It's about time you woke up."

She stared at the three-quarter profile of Daniel Metwater's face as he piloted the car down a paved highway, past a landscape of sagebrush fields and rocky cliffs. "What are you doing?" she asked, the words emerging as a strangled croak. She coughed and tried again. "Where are you taking me?"

"I haven't decided, exactly," he said. "I've been driving around, waiting for you to wake up and considering my options."

"Why are you so angry with me?" she asked. "What did I ever do to you?"

"It's not what you have done, but what you

potentially could do," he said. "The best way to handle a problem in your life is to address it before it becomes serious. You may recall a teaching I presented on that topic at the campfire circle one evening not too long ago."

He must have interpreted her frown as puzzlement. "Of course you don't remember," he said. "I always suspected you of not paying attention."

No one had paid attention to his nightly sermons—or what he called "teachings"—most of the time. Even the uber-faithful like Asteria would tune out after a while. Good looks and charisma could take a man a long way, but they weren't enough to cow two dozen healthy adults into hanging on to his every word night after night. But Michelle knew better than to anger Metwater by pointing this out. "What do you mean—what I could potentially do?" she asked.

He glanced up at her in the rearview mirror, then back at the road. "One of my gifts is reading people," he said. "I can almost always watch a new follower for a day or two and figure out what he or she is looking for from me, and I determine how to fill that need. It's what makes me a great leader."

A great manipulator, she thought.

"For instance, more than anything, Asteria wants a home and security. She wants to feel safe. I can give that to her and to her child."

"And in exchange, she gives you everything," Michelle blurted.

Metwater nodded. "The definition of a fair exchange is one in which each party receives what he or she wants, so I would say the exchange between Asteria and myself is infinitely fair. You, however, were much more difficult to read. I realized right away, of course, that this was because you were being deceptive."

He had realized no such thing. He had paid scarcely any attention to her in the first weeks after she and Greg came to the camp with Hunter. "If you thought I was such a liar, why did you let me stay?"

"Because I wanted to know what your game was. The best way to defeat an enemy is to know him."

"Was that one of your teachings, too?"

He laughed. "It was. Think of all the useful things you would have learned if you had been paying attention."

"So what do you think you know about me?" she asked.

"You're not malleable."

It wasn't the answer she had been expecting. "Why is that bad?" she asked.

"It isn't necessarily bad," he said. "I'm not malleable, either. But nonmalleable people don't mesh well in groups—unless they're the leader. I can't have someone in my group I can't control."

She somehow refrained from rolling her eyes. "Fine," she said. "So you kicked me out. End of story. Why kidnap me now?"

"You're too dangerous, especially now that you're in bed with the cops."

He had chosen that particular figure of speech on purpose, she was sure. "I don't care about you," she said. "I only care about David, and what he did to my sister."

"If you start digging around in David's past, it could come back to hurt me. I've come much too far to let that happen."

That made her curious, as he must have known it would. Which also meant he had no intention of letting her live long enough to dig further into his past. "Since we're baring our souls here," she said, "tell me the truth about what happened to Hunter. Where is he? What did you do to him?" Her voice broke on the last words, and she blinked hard, forcing back tears. She wouldn't break down in front of this arrogant jerk, no matter what.

"Some guys I knew in Chicago owed me a favor," he said. "They agreed to come down and babysit your little boy. You don't have to worry about him—he's all right."

Relief rocked her back in the seat, and she swayed, light-headed. Metwater wasn't the type to spare her feelings, so he must be telling the truth.

He slowed the car, then pulled onto the side of the road. She sat up straighter. The landscape hadn't changed—rolling stretches of sagebrush, rocky cliffs, achingly blue sky. "Why are we stopping?" she asked.

"I was thinking about my brother," he said. "About when they found his body. Have you ever seen someone who has drowned?"

She shook her head, then, realizing he couldn't see her, added, "No."

"Being in the water really messes up a body," he said. "By the time they found my brother, he was so disfigured no one could identify him. Dental records didn't help—we both have perfect teeth. They identified him based on a tattoo. I had to go in and look at it and bring pictures that showed him with the tattoo."

"Wh…why are you telling me this?"

"Because I wanted you to know that's what it's going to be like for you." He put the car in gear and turned back onto the highway. "Only a little farther now," he said. "I just have to find deep enough water."

WHEN EVERYONE WAS in their places around the motel, Ethan pulled out his phone. He texted Carmen.

Can you hear anything in there?

Some movement. The baby was crying a little bit ago, but he's quiet now.

I'm making my call now. Ethan replied.

Good luck.

He punched in the number Mr. Johanson had given him and waited. On the fifth ring, a man picked up. "Yeah?"

"This is Agent Ethan Reynolds with the Ranger Brigade. Is this Thad or Tom Smith?"

"What difference does it make to you? You all need to back off and leave us alone if you don't want this kid to get hurt."

"We don't want anyone to get hurt," Ethan

said. Though he kept his gaze fixed on the door to the room where the kidnappers waited, out of the corner of his eye he saw Simon and Michael inching along the front of the building, toward the door of the end room. "I'm sure you didn't plan for things to turn out this way." He needed to establish a connection with Smith and keep him on the line and distracted as long as possible.

"This was supposed to be a simple job," Smith said. "Snatch the kid and hold him for a few days."

A job. Meaning the Smiths were employees? "Whose idea was it to take the baby?" Ethan asked.

"Not mine. I wish I'd never laid eyes on the kid."

"So the person we should really be going after isn't you—it's the person who hired you."

"I'm not saying anything."

"Why? Because you're afraid of the person who hired you?"

"Because I'm not stupid. I roll over on him and I'll end up at the bottom of a river somewhere."

The door to the end room closed behind the two Rangers. Ethan hadn't heard anything to alert him that the Smiths were aware of their new neighbors. "Was the ransom note his idea or yours?" Ethan asked.

"What difference does it make?"

"I'm just trying to figure out what you want. If I know that, maybe we can come to an agreement that gets us both what we want."

"Hey, I didn't just fall off the turnip truck. No cop cares about what I want."

Ethan remembered Metwater's outrage when they'd shown him the ransom note. "Those idiots!" he had shouted. "How much did Daniel Metwater promise you for taking the boy?" he asked.

"Not nearly enough. Hey! I never said it was Metwater."

"You didn't have to. How much did he offer?"

Silence. "Come on," Ethan prodded. "Help me make my case against him and it will go better for you."

"Five thousand," Smith said. "We were just supposed to keep the kid for a few days while he taught some woman a lesson."

It wasn't enough that Metwater had beat up Michelle—he had to steal her baby, too. "But it took longer than you thought," Ethan prompted.

"Yeah. And the kid hardly shuts up. He cried all night last night. We hardly slept."

"That's rough." Ethan pretended to sympathize. "He sounds quiet now."

"He's asleep."

"You have a crib in there?" Ethan tried to picture where a baby bed might fit into the small room.

"We put some pillows in the bathtub and put him in there. He seems to like it, and we can shut the door if he starts wailing again."

Ethan's heart leaped at this news. He grabbed his notepad and scrawled a message to the commander. "Text Carmen that the baby is in the bathtub, asleep."

Ellison glanced at the note and nodded. Ethan forced his attention back to the call. "You must be pretty bored in there," he said. "What do you do to pass the time?"

"Mostly we watch TV and sleep." Someone mumbled in the background and Smith chuckled. "My brother says to tell you he's cleaning his gun."

"If you come out now, and leave the baby behind for us, I'll make sure the DA knows you cooperated," Ethan said.

Smith made a snorting sound. "We're not moving until we get a solid deal—none of this *maybe* business."

"I'll see what I can do," Ethan said. "I'll

need to make some calls and talk to a few people. In the meantime, can I get you anything—food, beer, diapers?"

"We're good."

Ethan ended the call and looked at Ellison. The commander gave him a thumbs-up. "Simon and Michael are in place," Ellison said. "They were able to open the door on their side while you were on the phone with Smith. We'll come in the front while they come in the side."

"We know they're armed," Ethan said. "They'll start shooting right away."

"We think we can overpower them before they know what hit them," Ellison said. "We're going to fire tear gas in before we go in. We'll have gas masks, but they won't."

"Neither will Hunter," Ethan said.

"Carmen is at the back window with Lance," Ellison said. "She thinks she can get in the window—which is already open a few inches. He'll boost her up and she'll go in and grab the baby and hand him out to Lance while the Smiths are dealing with their surprise visitors. The gas won't have had time to reach the bathroom yet, especially with the door closed."

Ethan nodded. It sounded like a good plan, but he knew too well that things could always go wrong.

Chapter Fifteen

"What's my role?" Ethan asked.

"Get Smith back on the phone," Ellison said. "Pump him for more information about Metwater's involvement. Get him worked up if you can—agitated and distracted. Try to get him to look out the window at you—that will put him farther from the connecting door when we go in."

Ethan nodded. All he had to do was keep his cool, and let the team do its job. "Do you need a minute?" Ellison asked.

"No, I'm good." He held up the phone. "I'm ready when you are."

"Go when Randall and I are in the room with Simon and Michael."

He waited while the commander added a helmet and shield to his riot gear. Ellison and Randall Knightbridge, who was similarly outfitted, slipped out of sight behind the motel office, then reappeared at the corner of the building. Moving stealthily, they made their way to the door of the end room and disappeared inside.

Ethan called the Smiths. Someone answered right away. The baby wailed in the background. "What?" Thad demanded.

"I need you to tell me more about Metwater," he said. "I need to be able to convince the DA that you can give us information we can't get anywhere else. I need him to see that you're too valuable to pass up the opportunity to get you on our side."

"Yeah, and if I tell you everything I know now, you won't need me at all," he said. "Tom, shut that kid up. I can't think!"

"He'll stop crying in a minute," Ethan said. "Try turning on the TV. They like to hear the voices."

"I'll try anything." After a moment the sound of a television came up. Miraculously, Hunter's crying stopped. "Hey, it worked!"

"Just leave him in the bathtub and he'll probably fall back asleep in a minute," Ethan said. In any case, the noise from the television would help cover up any sounds from the room next door. "I don't need much, I just need a little to make the DA happy. You mentioned Metwater's connections. What did you mean by that?"

"What do you think I mean?" Smith asked. "Chicago? Connections?"

"You mean the mob?" Ethan asked. "I thought his brother was the one who was tied up with the Mafia."

"That's what everybody thought, but they were all wrong."

"How do you know this?" Ethan asked.

"Uh-uh. I'm not going there. In fact, we're done talking."

"Don't hang up!" Ethan said. "Tell me about this woman Metwater wanted to teach a lesson. What was his beef with her?"

"Man, I don't know," Smith said. "All he told us was that we had to keep the kid out of sight for a few days until she learned her lesson. He said he'd give us five thousand bucks to babysit and that's all I needed to know."

"But then he didn't pay you."

"He didn't come through with the money and he couldn't tell me when the job would be over."

"So you decided to make the best of things and sent the ransom note," Ethan said. "That way, at least you'd get something out of the deal."

"That's about it. We had to cover our expenses, you know? And this way, the kid ended up back with his mother. We're not heartless."

"I can see that. And the DA will take that into considera—"

An explosion cut off his word. Shouting, and thuds. Ethan clutched the phone to his ear and stared at the front of the hotel, but the curtains to the Smiths' room remained closed, providing no clue about what was going on inside. Then two figures raced from behind the building. Carmen, followed by Lance, jogged along the far side of the parking lot to reach Ethan. She cradled a blanket-wrapped bundle to her chest and was grinning from ear to ear. "He's okay," she said, before Ethan could ask.

"We've got EMTs on the way," Lance said. "They'll take him to the hospital for a checkup. His mom can meet us there."

His mom. Ethan ended the call to the Smiths and punched in the number for his duplex. The phone rang and rang. "Michelle probably isn't answering because she thinks the call is for me," he said.

The door to the motel room burst open and a bearded young man with long brown hair stumbled out, his hands cuffed behind him, followed by Commander Ellison, and a second handcuffed man handled by Simon and Randall. They hustled the prisoners over to the cruisers and put them in the back seats.

Ellison pulled off his helmet and joined Ethan, Lance and Carmen, who was still holding Hunter. The baby was wailing, loudly, his face red from the effort. "I think he needs a bottle and a clean diaper," Carmen said as she jostled him in her arms. "I hope the EMTs come prepared."

"I tried to reach Michelle, but she's not answering the phone," Ethan said. "Maybe she's asleep."

Ellison clapped Ethan on the back. "Go give her the good news in person. Then you can bring her to the hospital to be reunited with her baby."

"What about Metwater?" Ethan asked.

"Marco and I are on our way to his camp now to arrest him," Ellison said. "His lawyers aren't going to get him off the hook on this one, I promise."

Ethan left, forcing himself to keep close to the speed limit. Sometimes in his job he got the opportunity to do something really good. This was one of those times. He couldn't wait to see Michelle's face when he told her they had found Hunter safe and sound. After so much in her life going wrong for her, this time things had gone right.

The setting sun painted the graying sky with streaks of pink and orange behind Ethan's duplex. Purple thunderclouds loomed in the distance, and the air was heavy with the promise of a storm. Ethan parked in the drive and strode up the walk, grinning in anticipation of sharing the good news about Hunter. But the damaged front door stopped him in his tracks. "Michelle!" he called.

When she didn't answer, he drew his weapon and approached cautiously. He nudged open the damaged door and stepped inside. Only dark, still air greeted him. Maybe Michelle was taking a nap, though he couldn't imagine she would sleep until she knew her son was safe.

He flipped on the light and started for the bedroom, but was only a few feet into the room when he stopped and stared at the overturned bar stool, shattered cup and scattered bits of plastic on the floor. Heart hammering, he knelt and put a fingertip to the coffee pooled among the shards of china. Cold. Then he spotted another dark puddle a foot from the coffee, and icy fear gripped him. He took the flashlight from his utility belt and played it across the stain, noting the syrupy burgundy-brown shimmer of blood.

"Michelle!" he shouted, and ran toward the bedroom. Empty. He checked the bathroom and the guest room, and looked into the tiny fenced backyard. Nothing. But he found her purse on the sofa, and her sweater on the peg by the door. Keys in one hand, cell phone in the other, he jogged back to the cruiser.

"Ellison." The commander's voice was crisp, warning the caller not to waste his time.

"Michelle's gone. The house is empty and there's sign of a struggle and blood on the floor."

"Stay there," Ellison ordered. "I'll send someone. Stay put until they get there."

"Yes, sir." Ethan slumped against the cruiser and stared toward the house. Where was he going to go, anyway? He had no idea where Michelle might be, or what had happened to her.

He stayed outside until a Ranger Brigade cruiser pulled over to the curb. Simon and Randall got out, along with Randall's police dog, Lotte. "The commander said something happened with Michelle," Randall said.

"I came home to tell her we'd found Hunter, and the house was empty," Ethan said. "There's an overturned chair, a broken coffee cup and a little bit of blood on the floor. Her purse is still there, and her sweater. I don't think she would have left without them if she had had the choice." He was surprised at how calm he sounded, how detached and businesslike, when inside his emotions were in turmoil.

"Let's take a look," Simon said, and led the way up the walk.

They took pictures and measurements, and searched the duplex for anything Ethan might have missed. Lotte sniffed Michelle's handbag and sweater and on the command "Find" trailed the scent to the end of the driveway. Simon found another spot of blood on the curb and took a sample for the lab.

"I'd say someone came in a car and she left with them," Simon said. "Either voluntarily or involuntarily."

"The blood tells me it was involuntary," Randall said.

"Who have we got watching Metwater?" Ethan asked.

Simon and Randall exchanged looks. "When the call came in about the hostage situation, the commander pulled me off that duty," Randall said. "Metwater didn't show any signs of going anywhere."

"Somebody should check if he's still in camp," Simon said.

"I'll do it," Ethan said.

"We'll run these samples to the lab and put out an APB for Michelle," Simon said. "And one for Metwater, too, in case he's done a runner."

"Hang in there," Randall said. "We'll find her."

Ethan nodded and climbed into his cruiser. He only hoped they found Michelle before it was too late. There hadn't been a lot of blood, but any at all was too much when it was someone you cared about.

Someone you loved. This was a heck of a time to realize he was in love with Michelle, but a crisis brought everything into clearer focus. Maybe there were more than a few reasons why the two of them shouldn't be together, but right now the only one that mattered was that it was tearing his heart out to think of her hurt or in need. He would do anything to save her—anything to be with her again. That was the kind of glue that kept people together in spite of their differences and difficulties, he thought. If only he had the chance to prove that theory to her.

He watched for signs of Michelle along the

road as he drove toward Metwater's camp, scrutinizing every car and truck and camper that passed. When he turned off the paved road, he pushed the cruiser as fast as he dared, rattling over washboarded sections and bouncing over potholes with a force that threatened to shake parts of the vehicle—or parts of him—loose.

At last, he screeched to a halt at Metwater's compound and jogged up the trail to the camp. He bounded up the steps to Metwater's motor home and pounded hard on the door. "Open up, police!" he shouted.

"He's not there."

Ethan turned to see a shirtless young man with a shaved head and a torso full of colorful tattoos. "What did you say?" he asked.

"He's not there," the man said. "He left about an hour ago—maybe a little more."

"Where did he go?"

The man shrugged. "Don't know."

"Was he by himself?"

The man considered the question. "Yeah. I think he was."

That was probably the best answer Ethan was going to get. "How did he leave?" he asked. "Did someone drive him?" That was

Metwater's usual habit—to have someone else drive him on his errands.

"Nah. He was driving that old car of Starfall's."

"What's your name?" Ethan asked.

"Roscoe."

He didn't offer a last name, but Ethan didn't need to know it. "You're the mechanic, right?" he asked. "The guy who salvages junk cars?"

Roscoe looked wary. "How do you know that?"

"Starfall mentioned that you'd worked on her car for her."

"Yeah. It's old, but it's in pretty good shape."

"You ever work on other cars—for people other than Family members?" Ethan asked.

"I could. Why? You got one that needs fixing?"

"I'm wondering if you ever crossed paths with guys who were bringing in cars from town," Ethan said. "Stripping them for parts, or maybe altering them before moving them on to other locations."

Roscoe took a step back. "You're talking about stolen cars." He shook his head. "Nuh-uh. I don't mess with that."

"But you might know someone who does? Someone else here in camp?" Ethan looked around—the few people who had been out and about when he arrived had vanished, though he suspected more than one pair of eyes watched him from the cover of tents and trailers.

"Nobody here in camp," Roscoe said. "The Prophet wouldn't allow it. He's always talking to us about being honest and respecting other people's property."

"Fine. Nobody here in camp. But somebody has been boosting cars in town and stripping them down out here on public land." He gave Roscoe a hard look. "If I find out you know who it is and you don't tell me, I'll have to assume it's because you're involved. A guy like you, with mechanical ability, would be a real asset to an operation like that. And if you already have a record..." The last point was a guess on Ethan's part, but an educated one, since some of Roscoe's artwork looked like jailhouse tats.

Roscoe paled. "All I know is a couple of guys named Smith asked me if I'd be interested in working for them."

Smith again. "Describe them."

"Young. Brown hair, kind of long. Brothers, I think, but the younger one takes the lead, does most of the talking."

"Any first names?" Ethan asked.

Roscoe shook his head. "I never heard any."

"How did you meet them?" Ethan asked.

"They came up to me at the salvage yard about a month ago. I had a load of scrap I'd hauled in to sell. Not cars, but a couple of old washing machines, some couch springs—you wouldn't believe the trash people dump out here."

"And this Smith guy just walked up to you?"

"Yeah. He said he'd heard I was good with cars and he needed someone like me to do some work for him."

"Did he say who recommended you?"

Roscoe frowned. "I didn't ask. I figure it was somebody I knew on the inside. I told him I didn't do that stuff anymore—that I was straight and going to stay that way."

"What did he say to that?" Ethan asked.

"He laughed." Roscoe scowled. "Made me mad. I told him where to go and got in my truck and left."

"So he never actually said he was stealing cars?" Ethan tried not to show his disappointment.

"He didn't have to. I know the types. Not too long after that, the guy who runs the salvage yard, Frankie, told me the cops were on the lookout for a car theft ring."

"You ever see the Smith brothers again?" Ethan asked. "They ever come by to visit the Prophet?"

"No way! I'm pretty sure that's why they laughed at me. When I told them I'd gone straight, I told them I was following the Prophet and he didn't hold with stealing. When people don't understand religion, the easiest way to put it down is to laugh at it."

Or maybe they had been laughing because they knew how wrong Roscoe was to believe the Prophet was so lily-white and honest. "Any idea where they're operating?" Ethan asked.

Roscoe shook his head. "I don't know and I don't want to know."

"They boosted my mother's car yesterday," Ethan said. "Brand-new Accord. She's pretty upset about it."

"Aw, dude, I'm sorry," Roscoe said. "I hope she had good insurance. These guys will have it stripped down or driven off to Mexico within twenty-four hours. I mean, I never saw their operation, but they struck me as pros. The name of the game in that business is speed— get the evidence off the street so you can't be linked with it and caught."

"Except you were caught," Ethan guessed.

Roscoe surprised him with a grin. "Yeah,

but only because I got greedy. I boosted a sweet Corvette and thought I could give it a new paint job and hang on to it. Stupid. But for the best, too. Otherwise, I might never have seen the light, you know?"

Ethan nodded. "Thanks for telling me what you know about the Smiths."

"Sorry about your mom's car," he said. "If you see Starfall, tell her I said hi. And I hope they find her kid."

"We found Hunter," Ethan said. "But now Michelle—Starfall—is missing."

"No!" Roscoe shook his head. "Some people sure have bad luck."

"Luck didn't have anything to do with it," Ethan said. "We think she might be with Daniel Metwater." He was careful not to say he thought she had been abducted. He didn't want anyone to think their Prophet was being accused of anything and needed protecting.

"Maybe she's trying to talk him into taking her back," Roscoe said. "I bet he will, if she has the right attitude. He only kicked her out because she needed a little tough love. We all do, sometimes."

Ethan didn't bother correcting the young man. He handed Roscoe one of his cards. "Call me if you hear anything more about the car thieves—or if you see Starfall."

"She in some kind of trouble with the cops?" Roscoe asked, studying the business card.

"We just want to make sure she's okay," Ethan said.

He debated questioning others but decided not to waste any more time. He raced back to his cruiser. As soon as he was in cell coverage again, he called in to Ranger Brigade Headquarters. Simon answered the phone. "What have you got?" he asked.

"Metwater left camp more than an hour ago. He was driving Michelle's old car. The maroon Chevy."

"Yeah, I know it," Simon said. "We'll put out a bulletin to watch for it. Anything else?"

"I talked to a guy named Roscoe. He's the group's mechanic, makes extra money selling salvage metal. He said a couple of guys named Smith—brothers—approached him about working for them parting out stolen cars."

"Another side project for Metwater, or their own idea?" Simon asked.

"Roscoe thought Metwater didn't know anything about it, but he comes across as a true believer in the Prophet."

"I'll see what I can get out of the Smiths,"

Simon said. "See if they knew anything about Metwater's plans for Michelle. Where are you now?"

"About fifteen miles from headquarters. I'm going to patrol around here for a while, see what I can spot."

"Good idea," Simon said. "Keep an eye on the weather. We're supposed to have a storm coming in—could bring flash flooding."

Ethan looked out at the dark clouds massed in the dusky sky. Wind bent the trees along the side of the road. "I'll be careful," he said, and ended the call.

He headed toward the lake, away from Ranger Headquarters. Where was Metwater most likely to go? He had no idea. For all he had studied and observed the phony Prophet, he knew very little about how the man thought. He called the commander. "Simon updated me about the situation," Ellison said. "Have you learned anything new?"

"No, sir. Are you still with the Smith brothers?"

"I am."

"Ask them if they know of anyone else who was helping Metwater—anyone not in his *family*," Ethan said. "Ask them if he ever talked about what he would do to Michelle. I'm trying to figure out what he's up to."

"Will do. I'll let you know as soon as I find out anything."

"Yes, sir." He ended the call and gripped the steering wheel tighter. All he needed was a clue—some little lead that would send him in the right direction. Metwater could be halfway to Denver by now—or very nearby, down one of the countless side roads that wound through the wilderness area. Ethan was tempted to turn off onto one of those roads, but he needed to stay in cell phone range in order to wait for the commander's return call.

Michelle was a survivor. He needed to remember that. She had been through so much already—more than most people could endure. Yet she had kept going. She would do everything in her power to stay alive for her son.

His phone rang and he snatched it up. "Hello?"

"The Smiths aren't talking," Commander Ellison said. "They're waiting for their attorney to show up, but he's already advised them not to speak with us."

"I'm going to take a look in the country around the camp," Ethan said. "Metwater knows that area best, so he might stick to familiar ground." What he didn't say—what he knew the commander was also thinking—was that if Metwater planned to kill Michelle, he would know places to hide the body where it would never be found.

Ethan ended the call and turned the cruiser around, headed for the turnoff to Metwater's camp at the base of Mystic Mesa. As he passed a dirt turnoff that led down toward the lake, he thought he saw a burgundy-colored sedan shrouded in a cloud of dust.

He braked hard, mind racing. Had the car really been Michelle's old beater, or was his imagination playing tricks on him? He swung onto the narrow road and gunned the cruiser, fishtailing wildly as he struggled to keep up with the vehicle ahead. All he could see now was the occasional glow of brake lights and the dust rising like mist in the glow of his headlights.

He cut the lights, relying on the dim remnants of daylight to guide him. He didn't want whoever was in that car to realize he was following. Light flashed on water, and he braked as he realized they were almost to the lake. He pulled to the side of the road and parked, letting the other car drive on down to the shore. He took out his phone to call in his location and suppressed a groan at the message that he had no service.

Wind buffeted him as he stepped out of the cruiser, bringing with it the scent of rain and damp sage. Jagged lightning tore the sky on the far side of the lake, and the headlights from the first car showed whitecaps on the dark water.

Ethan crept toward the parked car, shrinking back into the shadows when the driver's door opened. Metwater climbed out, then opened the back door and pulled someone out. Michelle fell to her knees, her hands tied behind her back, and Metwater hauled her up roughly. Ethan couldn't see her that well in the growing darkness, but he recognized the tangle of brown curls around her face, and the defiant posture with which she faced her captor.

He debated going back to the cruiser for his rifle, but taking the time to retrieve it might mean the difference between life and death for Michelle. He didn't think Metwater had brought her here at this time of evening to go swimming. Ethan moved forward down the slope toward the pair by the water.

A rock shifted beneath him and he fell, skidding down the slope. He rolled, drawing his weapon as bullets thudded into the dirt where a fraction of a second before he had lain. Michelle screamed and Ethan peered from behind a log where he had sought cover in time to see Metwater grab her by the hair and pull her in front of him. Now Ethan couldn't fire on Metwater without endangering her.

Metwater dragged Michelle toward the water lapping at the shore. She tried to pull away, kicking at him, but he held her fast and she slipped in the mud. He shoved her hard into the lake, holding her under the surface. If Ethan didn't act quickly, Metwater was going to drown her. He tried to aim his pistol at Metwater's back, but the Prophet's movements made it impossible to focus on the target.

Michelle had stopped fighting and lay still under the water. Enraged, Ethan grabbed up a piece of driftwood and charged toward Metwater, swinging the stick like a club. He struck Metwater on the side of the head, driving him away from Michelle. Ethan lunged into the water, groping for her hand. He found it and dragged her up, hauling her to shore just as Metwater leaped on him.

Ethan struggled to his feet and drew his weapon. "No!" Metwater roared and struck his arm hard, jolting the pistol loose. It landed in the lake with a splash and Metwater grabbed

Ethan's shoulders, trying to force him down into the water. The two men grappled, slipping in the mud and gravel.

"Run!" Ethan screamed at Michelle. She was on the shore on all fours, coughing violently.

Metwater was on top of Ethan now, one hand around Ethan's throat, choking him, the other grappling for his gun at his hip. Ethan fought for breath, struggling to remain conscious, to keep fighting long enough for Michelle to get away. Metwater had his own pistol out now, the barrel pressed against Ethan's forehead. He closed his eyes, waiting for the end.

Then Metwater's grasp on him loosened, and the Prophet groaned and staggered to his feet. Ethan struggled to rise also as Metwater turned toward Michelle, who stood a short distance away, the stick of driftwood in her hand. Metwater lunged toward her, and Ethan leaped on his back, his arm around the Prophet's throat, choking him. "Run!" he shouted at Michelle again, and this time she listened, taking off into the brush alongside the lakeshore.

Ethan tightened his grip on Metwater, squeezing hard, until the other man stopped fighting. He loosened his hold, intending to put Metwater in cuffs, but before he could reach his utility belt, Metwater turned on him once more. Face contorted by rage, he shoved Ethan away from him.

Ethan staggered back, struggling to keep his footing. Metwater scooped up his pistol and aimed it at Ethan, who only had time to dive behind a currant bush before the bullet thudded into the dirt to his right. He scrambled backward, seeking better cover, but Metwater relentlessly pursued. With no weapon and little cover, Ethan's only chance was to outrun the Prophet, and pray that the bullets that rained after him didn't find their target.

He ran hard, feet sending up sprays of gravel, zigzagging among the brush and driftwood that crowded this part of the lakeshore. Metwater stopped firing, though Ethan thought he heard the Prophet pounding along the shore after him.

"Ethan, here!"

He looked to the side and spotted Michelle standing at the edge of the water, beckoning him. As he drew closer, he saw that she held on to the bow of a battered green kayak. "He can't get to us if we're out on the water," she said, shoving a paddle into his hand and preparing to climb into the boat.

"There's a storm coming up," Ethan said,

looking up at the angry clouds barely visible against the blackening sky.

"There's nowhere else to go," she said, already in the boat. "Nowhere to hide, no way to get away from him. I promise you, he won't give up. At least this way we have a chance."

They would have a chance if they could get back to his cruiser, but to do that they would have to negotiate a steep bluff in the dark, with Metwater in pursuit. Still, Ethan didn't like their chances on the water. He was about to tell Michelle as much when a bullet clipped the rock to his right, sending chips of granite flying. He glanced back over his shoulder and saw Metwater closing in.

"Hurry!" Michelle pleaded.

He stepped into the boat and pushed off with the paddle. He could feel her paddling also, and together they pulled away from shore. In the gathering dusk, he could make out a point of land to their left, and headed around this, hoping to get out of sight of Metwater as quickly as possible. Once Ethan was sure they were safe, they could beach the kayak and make their way back up to the road and, eventually, to his cruiser and safety.

Metwater shouted from the shore, his words swallowed up by the rising wind and the slap of waves against the kayak's fiberglass hull. A dozen more strokes with the paddles and Ethan couldn't hear him at all—or see the shore, or much of anything else, but dark sky against dark water. The sensation was eerie and disorienting. He kept paddling, afraid if they stopped the wind would blow them back to Metwater, but he stared into the darkness, trying to make out some landmark to steer by.

"I don't hear him anymore," Michelle said.

"No. But like you said—he doesn't give up. He's still out there."

As if to prove him right, light glowed from shore—the headlights of the car, twin spots shooting across the water. But the kayak was beyond the reach of the light. "What are we going to do now?" she asked.

"We have to get farther down the shore," Ethan said. "If we get around this point of land, we should be able to come into shore again. He'll probably still be looking for us, but he won't know where we are."

"Then I guess we'd better get paddling."

Chapter Sixteen

They paddled, but the wind was picking up and though Ethan couldn't see anything in the darkness, it didn't feel to him as if they were making much progress. Lightning streaked across the sky, revealing the rocky shoreline several hundred yards away—the storm had blown them even farther than he had thought. Thunder crashed, and rain began to lash them, icy needles stinging bare skin.

"It doesn't feel like we're getting anywhere!" Michelle shouted above the roar of the storm.

"Keep paddling!" he shouted. 'We've got to get to shore." Waves slapped against the fiberglass hull, buffeting them, making the boat more and more difficult to control. Rain continued to pound down, cold water puddling around his feet in the open boat.

The boat turned sideways and waves threatened to swamp them. Water streaming into his eyes, Ethan fought to turn the boat into the gale. The boat rose, bow out of the water altogether, and then they were falling, tossed up and over, falling through the darkness into the icy, churning water.

Michelle fought her way to the surface, sputtering and thrashing as yet another cold wave engulfed her. "Ethan!" she shouted, water streaming down her face and into her eyes. She struggled to stay afloat, looking wildly around her.

"Over here!"

She spun around and saw Ethan waving to her from where he clung to the kayak, which was upright once more. She swam to him and joined him in clinging to the boat. Neither spoke for a long moment as the waves tossed them about. Chill seeped into her, and her teeth began to chatter. "We should get back in the boat," she said.

"It's too full of water."

She dipped her hand down into the boat and realized he was right—the body of the kayak was almost filled with water. She wanted to scream in frustration. After everything she had been through, she wasn't going to die of exposure here in the middle of a lake. "What are we going to do?" she asked as lightning flashed. For a fraction of a second, she caught sight of Ethan's face, pale but determined, across from her.

"Can you get on my side of the boat and kick?" he shouted above the storm. "I thought I saw land up ahead."

Carefully, she maneuvered around the boat, terrified that if she let go the waves would sweep her away. After agonizing minutes she positioned herself next to him. "Kick hard!" he shouted, and she put her head down and kicked.

They had been at it long enough for her legs to begin aching. Her fingers were cramped from clinging to the kayak. She was about to tell Ethan it was hopeless when her foot struck something. Then her other foot touched bottom. Ethan was already standing and reaching for her. They clung to each other, staggering out of the water, pushing the waterlogged kayak in front of them.

When they were all the way out of the water, Michelle sank to her knees, struggling to breathe, trying to ignore the shivers that rocked her. Ethan tugged at her arm. "Come on," he said. "We have to find shelter and a way to keep warm."

She didn't see how they were going to find any of that in the darkness, but just then he switched on a flashlight. The beam sent a thin disk of light across the landscape, showing driftwood and scrub brush and the kind of debris that often washed up at lakes—fishing lures and water bottles and beer cans. "I guess this thing really is waterproof," Ethan said as he helped her to her feet. He played the beam over the area around them, then pointed inland. "Let's get into those trees. Maybe we can make some kind of shelter."

Make it out of what? she wanted to ask, but since the alternative was standing here in a downpour by herself, she followed him.

A few yards inland they found more trash—some boards and what looked like an old tarp. Ethan spread out the boards over the wet ground, then shook out the tarp and draped it over them. She told herself not to think what might be on that tarp. It was raining so hard the worst of the grime would have been washed off, right?

Ethan wrapped one arm around her and pulled her close. "When the rain lets up a little, I'll try to start a fire," he said.

"Let me guess," she said. "You were a Boy Scout."

"An Eagle Scout," he said.

"Of course." She rested her head on his shoulder and closed her eyes. "I don't care what you were—you saved me. Metwater was going to kill me. And then I thought he was going to kill you." Her voice broke on the last words. The thought that he could have died while trying to rescue her shook her.

"I wasn't going to let him kill you." He rubbed her shoulder. "Hunter is waiting to see you."

She was so numb it took a moment for his words to sink in. She stared at him, even though she could only see the dim outline of his face in the darkness. "Do you really have him? Is he all right?"

"He's fine. We took him to the hospital as a precaution, but he's fine."

"Where? What happened? Who?"

He chuckled. "Hold on and I'll tell you the whole story. It was just like you suspected—Metwater was behind it all." She listened, stunned, as he told about the Smith brothers and the little motel where they attempted to hold Hunter hostage. He described the rescue in the briefest terms, but even so it sounded incredibly brave and daring to her. "I can't believe you found him." She threw her arms around him and kissed his cheek. "I can't ever thank you enough."

"You don't have to thank me." He snuggled her close again. "I'm glad we were able to find him."

"And now here we are, stuck who knows where."

"In the morning we'll be able to figure out where we are and go for help," he said. "Hunter is safe until then."

"Except that Daniel Metwater is still out there," she said. "When he finds out you have the Smith brothers, and I've escaped, he'll be furious."

"He won't get past the hospital staff and the deputies who are guarding Hunter," Ethan said. "And we've alerted all the local law enforcement agencies to be on the lookout for him. He won't be able to go far."

"He has a lot of money and a lot of friends," she said. "He can do a lot more than you think he can."

"How did he get hold of you?" Ethan asked. "What happened?"

"He came to the house. He said he followed me from Ranger Headquarters the day before. I guess he had been watching, waiting to catch me alone. Anyway, he was furious. He hit me and I guess I passed out. When I woke up in the car, he started talking about drowning—about what it did to a body, and how he had to identify his brother based on a tattoo." She shuddered, remembering the horror of his words. "I was terrified I was going to die."

"Why was he angry with you?"

"He said I knew too much and could get him in trouble. I tried to tell him I was only interested in proving that his brother had murdered Cass, but he said David *hadn't* murdered her—that he hadn't done any of the bad things people thought he had. He said that was one thing David and Cass had in common. It didn't make sense, really."

"What do you know that could get him in trouble?" Ethan asked.

"I can't think of anything. All I have are those news articles I printed off the internet. Everything in them is public knowledge."

"If David Metwater isn't guilty of the crimes people think he committed, maybe it's because Daniel Metwater did them," Ethan said.

"But that can't be right," she said. "Daniel was always the good brother. He ran the family business. He bailed David out of jail. He sat on charitable boards. The articles in the scrapbook were full of stuff like that. He couldn't have faked *all* of that."

"He's managed to fake an identity as a peace-loving prophet who is only interested in spiritual matters," Ethan said.

"When I first came to live with him and his followers, I thought that was true," she said. "I never believed that he could predict the future, or that he had all the answers, the way Asteria and some of the others believe, but when he talked about how his brother's death had led him to seek answers in a simpler life, I thought he was telling the truth. And I saw how he had made a difference in people's lives. There are members of the Family who are former drug addicts or cons, and they turned their lives around because of Daniel Metwater. I thought if he did that much good, how could he be bad? I guess I was as naive as everyone else."

"You weren't naive," Ethan said. "He's an expert at deceiving others, which tells me it's a talent he's been honing for a long time. When he's back in custody, I think it will be worth digging deeper into his past activities."

"If you can find him," she said.

"We'll find him," Ethan said. "He's arrogant and thinks he's above the law—that will work in our favor." He lifted the tarp a little.

"The rain has stopped. I'll see about starting that fire now."

He left and she felt bereft—colder both physically and emotionally. When they were back in the real world—when Hunter was safely with her again and it was time for her to move on to whatever the next phase of her life might be—how would she find the strength to say goodbye to this man who had come to mean so much to her?

Ethan had been kind to her—maybe he even had some feelings for her. But he had a full life already—he had an important job and friends and family—all the things she had never had. She didn't even know how she would fit into that kind of world.

ETHAN MANAGED TO find enough dry wood and tinder to get a good blaze going. He settled next to Michelle in front of it, and extended his hands to warm them. "That should help dry us off and thaw us out," he said.

"I'm impressed." She held her own hands out to the flames. "You really were a good Eagle Scout."

"Don't be too impressed." He pulled a lighter from his pocket. "I had this."

"Ethan Reynolds, don't tell me you're a secret smoker."

"Nope." He pocketed the lighter once more. "It's part of the emergency kit we all carry—first-aid kit, whistle, pocketknife, et cetera." He patted a pouch on his belt. "First time I've ever had to use it, though."

"You're still a good Eagle Scout," she said. "Isn't their motto 'be prepared'?"

"If I was that good, I'd have some emergency food stashed somewhere," he said. As if in agreement, his stomach growled.

"Food would be nice, but we won't starve before morning," she said.

"You're right." He patted her shoulder. "Why don't we lie down and try to get some rest?"

"I'm too keyed up to sleep," she said. "I've been worried about Hunter for so long—knowing he's safe I feel so much lighter—nothing else that has happened to me matters now that I know my baby is safe and I'm going to see him again."

"I'll admit I'm keyed up, too." He studied the inky sky—clouds still covered the stars. "As soon as it's daylight we need to get out of here, and we need to start searching for Metwater and bring him in."

"I don't want to think about Metwater anymore tonight," she said. "I don't even want to think about tomorrow." She slipped her arms around his waist and cuddled against him. "Now that I'm dry and getting warmer, I think we should take advantage of this time alone."

He caressed her shoulder, enjoying the feel of her soft curves against him. "Oh, yeah? What did you have in mind?"

"This." She pulled his face to his and kissed him, the crush of her warm mouth to his banishing the last chill from his body. He gathered her to him, lying back and pulling her down with him so that her soft breasts pressed against his chest, her body heavy against his arousal. She opened her mouth to deepen the kiss and he plunged his tongue into her, tasting warm sweetness. Forget food, this was what he needed right now—to taste and devour her, to quench the hunger that had been building in him ever since he spent that first night in her bed. He didn't believe he would ever get tired of making love to Michelle.

He caressed her bottom, then slid his hands up her back and around to cup her breasts. She arched against him and growled out a sound of pleasure. Fighting his own impatience, he pulled off her shirt, then made quick work of her bra. His lips closed around one taut nipple and her low moan pierced him, desire hot and urgent.

He shifted to focus on her other breast, but she slid down, out of his reach, and looked down into his eyes, firelight playing across the side of her face. "Officer, we need to get you out of this uniform," she said.

"I've heard some women find the uniform sexy," he teased.

"I prefer you naked." She started unbuttoning his shirt. "I want to feel skin against my skin, not some pointy badge."

His badge didn't have any points, but he got the message. And skin-to-skin contact sounded good to him, too.

It took a few moments for both of them to peel out of their still-damp clothing. He spread the clothes over the tarp to form a makeshift bed; then they lay down side by side, stroking and caressing, exchanging long, drugging kisses, letting the need build again. He threaded his fingers through the riot of curls around her face. "You have the most amazing hair," he said.

She laughed. "This mess? I thought men were into long blond tendrils or raven tresses or silky red hair. My hair is plain old brown, and there's no style to it—it just grows and kinks."

"I like it," he said. "It's a little wild—like you."

"Oh, you like wild, do you?"

"I do."

"I can show you wild." She moved over him, hands on either side of his head, straddling his torso. When she took him inside her, he let out a low groan, and when she began to move in a slow, sensual dance, he lost focus. She took his hand, and guided it down between them. He licked his thumb, then began to stroke, feeling her tighten around him. He felt very close to the edge, and tried to pull back, but she increased the tempo of her thrusts, driving them both up and over. She came with a loud cry, bucking hard, taking him deep inside her. His own release overwhelmed him, and he clung to her, riding the wave until he was utterly spent.

She pressed her forehead to his, and he felt more than saw her smile. "Wild enough for you?" she whispered.

His answer was a kiss, one he didn't break as she eased off him and moved to his side once more. He broke the contact and looked down into her eyes. "You're amazing," he whispered.

She closed her eyes. "Yeah. Amazing."

He wanted to tell her he loved her, but caution held him back. He didn't want her to freak out or push him away. She hadn't had much love in her life, as far as he could tell. And too many people who were supposed to love her hadn't followed through on that love. Words weren't going to be enough for her.

She had her baby and a new life to get back to. He couldn't see her sticking around for a cop, of all people. He was the kind of man who liked to look after people—maybe too much, his mother might say.

She was a woman who valued her independence, who sometimes chafed under his overprotectiveness.

She fell asleep in his arms. He watched the firelight play across her face. She looked younger in repose, the tension around her eyes and jaw relaxed. He wanted to take away all the reasons for that tension, to show her that she didn't have to bear all her burdens alone. But after being on her own for so long, did she even have it in her to trust? She was like the feral cats his mother fed. She could care for them, but they would never come inside and live with her. They would never make her world theirs, or allow her to be more than a peripheral part of their lives.

MICHELLE WOKE TO bright sun in her eyes and a soft breeze across her bare skin. She blinked, then sat up, hastily pulling up the shirt she had apparently been using as a makeshift cover. In daylight, their camp looked even more pitiful than she had imagined it last night—a dirty blue tarp and some pieces of plywood beside a campfire of driftwood.

A rustling to her right set her heart to thudding and she searched in vain for someplace to hide. What if Metwater had found them? What if he had already hurt Ethan and was coming for her?

Then Ethan stepped from the underbrush—bare-chested and barefoot, uncombed hair and a day's stubble transforming him into sexy backwoodsman. She hugged her knees to her chest and grinned at him. If it wasn't for Hunter and her growling stomach, she wouldn't have minded spending another day or two camped out with this hot cop. But she needed to keep playing it cool. She couldn't let him see how much he had come to mean to her. She didn't do needy.

"I don't suppose you found any coffee back in there?" she asked.

"Nope." He crouched beside the remains of last night's campfire. "But I think I've figured out where we are."

"Oh?" She pulled the shirt around and started to put it on, then realized it was his.

"I would say keep it—it looks better on you," he said. "But I might need it." He handed her her shirt and, aware of him watching, she began to dress.

"Where are we?" she asked as she hooked her bra.

"We're on an island in the lake, maybe half a mile from shore."

Her heart sank. "No way can I swim half a mile," she said.

"We still have the kayak," he said. "In daylight, with calm water, we shouldn't have any trouble getting to shore. From there we can walk to a store or a marina with a phone."

She shuddered at the memory of the terrifying last moments in that kayak, but nodded. She had done plenty of things in her life that had frightened or repelled her—she ought to be good at it by now.

"As soon as you dress we can leave," he said. "I'm hoping we end up near someplace with coffee. And food."

She stood and shoved her feet into her still-damp tennis shoes. "Just give me a minute to, um, freshen up in the woods," she said.

"Oh, sure. I'll finish dressing myself and get the boat ready."

She slipped into the underbrush, searching for a spot that was well out of sight. When she was finished, she ran fingers through her hair and smiled as she remembered what Ethan had said last night. All her life she had envied women with more manageable hair, but maybe hers wasn't so bad after all.

"Police! Keep your hands where we can see them!"

Fear replaced contentment as the man's voice, sharp and commanding, cut the peace of the morning. Scarcely daring to breathe, Michelle tiptoed to the edge of the woods and peered out.

Ethan, still shirtless and barefoot, hands in the air, faced two uniformed men with guns drawn. The men were very young, and she didn't recognize the uniforms. They also looked nervous, which made the weapons in their hands look that much more dangerous.

"He's got a gun," one of the men said, a blond. He nudged something with his foot, which she realized must have been Ethan's gun belt, which was lying on the tarp with the rest of his clothes.

"My ID is in my back pocket," Ethan said. "I can show you—"

"Don't move!" the blond ordered. He bent and scooped up the gun belt. "You need to come with us," he said. "And don't try to make trouble."

Chapter Seventeen

The two Forest Service employees were young and nervous, Ethan thought. A dangerous combination. Better to cooperate with them now—and enjoy their embarrassment later when they realized what a mistake they had made. He kept his hands up and his eyes focused on them, and prayed that Michelle would stay hidden.

"What do you think you're doing? For goodness' sake, he's a cop."

Of course Michelle wouldn't stay hidden, any more than she would have backed down if someone tried to intimidate her. Wasn't that one of the things he loved about her? But as the two men focused their attention on her, Ethan couldn't help wishing she was a little more subdued.

She stood at the edge of the clearing, hands

on her hips, hair a wild nimbus around her face. "He's part of the Ranger Brigade and he saved my life, so you need to put those guns away," she said, reminding him of a mother scolding a pair of little boys with water pistols instead of real weapons.

The Forest Service badges looked back at Ethan. "Is she telling the truth?" the dark-haired one asked.

"Yes. If you'll let me get out my ID, I'll prove it," Ethan said.

"All right," the blond said. "But do it slowly. No sudden moves."

"Of course." He carefully reached back and took out his wallet and flipped it open to his badge and ID.

Both men leaned forward to scrutinize it, and a red flush worked its way up the blond's neck. He holstered his weapon. "Sorry," he said. "We didn't realize you were a fed."

"We got a message to be on the lookout for a dangerous escaped felon," the dark-haired young man said as he, too, put away his gun. "They said he might have killed a cop and be hiding out in the area. When we saw you out here by yourself—where no one is supposed to be—we thought you were him."

"He killed a cop?" Ethan asked. Was this Metwater they were talking about, or someone else? "What cop?"

The two exchanged looks. "An FBI agent, I think," the blond said. "And he may have murdered someone else. And he kidnapped a baby."

"We're talking a really bad dude," his partner said.

That sounded like Metwater, all right, Ethan thought. Though he hoped they were wrong about the cop part. The other FBI agent on the Ranger Brigade was the commander. He pushed aside the thought. He couldn't dwell on those worries. "I think we're looking for the same guy," he said. He picked up his shirt and put it on. "How did you guys get out here?"

"We have a boat." The blond motioned toward the water. "We're assigned to patrol this area. Mostly we ticket drunken boaters or folks who don't have life jackets. This is about the most exciting thing to happen since we've been working here."

"How long have you been working here?" Ethan asked as he slipped on his gun belt. Even though he had lost his gun in the fight with Metwater, the belt was part of his uniform.

The two exchanged glances and the blond went red again. "About two months," he mumbled.

Michelle joined them. "If you have a boat, you can get us out of here," she said.

"Uh, sure, we can take you." The blond looked around. "How did you get here anyway?"

"It's a long story." Ethan clapped him on the back. "And it involves that fugitive you're looking for. We'd be grateful if you could take us back to my vehicle."

"Sure." He turned to Michelle. "Ma'am, are you an officer, too?"

She laughed. "No. I'm an innocent bystander." Without a look back, she strolled past the three men, headed toward shore. Ethan grinned and followed.

Thirty minutes later the Forest Service Rangers—Clint and Joe—delivered them to Ethan's cruiser—which was cordoned off with crime scene tape and surrounded by Rangers. Marco Cruz looked up from taking measurements and grinned. "I'll bet you've got a heck of a story to tell," he said, coming over and clapping Ethan on the back.

Lance joined them. "We saw the blood and

the signs of struggle and feared the worst," he said.

That explained the story the Forest Service Rangers had given him about a dead FBI guy, Ethan thought.

"Daniel Metwater was trying to drown me, and Ethan saved me," Michelle said. "We got away, but we ended up spending the night on an island in the lake. Then these two gentlemen found us this morning." She introduced the two officers, diplomatically omitting the fact that they had mistaken Ethan for a fugitive.

"It's a long story," Ethan said. "You can read my report later, but what I want to know now is have you found Metwater?"

"No," Marco said. "We've been watching the camp, but he hasn't shown up."

"His name and face and a description of the car are all over the area," Lance said. "We'll find him."

"We will," Ethan said. "He hasn't got the ego to lie low for long."

"I don't care about Metwater right now," Michelle said. "I need to see my son. Where is Hunter?"

"I'll take you to the hospital to see him," Ethan said.

"He's doing fine," Lance said, correctly interpreting her worried look. "The hospital was a safe place to keep him until the two of you could be reunited."

Since Ethan's cruiser was covered in fingerprint dust, he borrowed Marco's. As they headed toward Montrose, Michelle fidgeted, unable to sit still. "Tell me the truth," she said. "Is Hunter really all right? Those men didn't hurt him, did they? If they did—"

"As far as we can tell, they took good care of him," Ethan said. "And he's too young to remember anything. He'll be fine."

He parked in the visitors' lot at the hospital and led her in the front entrance and up to the pediatric floor. He was surprised to see his mom, in pink scrubs and white clogs, cuddling a baby to her shoulder. Even more surprising was her hair, which was cut fashionably short and streaked with blond.

"Hunter!" At the sound of Michelle's voice, the baby lifted his head and began to flail his arms. Ethan's mother turned, and when she saw Ethan and Michelle, a smile bloomed on her face.

"He definitely knows his mama," she said, walking toward them.

"Michelle, you remember my mom, Nancy," Ethan said.

But Michelle scarcely acknowledged either of them. She was pulling Hunter into her arms, covering his head with kisses and making little cooing noises. "Oh, my sweet baby," she murmured, closing her eyes and rocking Hunter against her.

Nancy touched Ethan's arm. "Let's give them a moment alone," she said.

He followed her out into the hall. "Mom, what did you do to your hair?" he asked, unable to stop staring at her.

She put one hand to her head. "Do you like it?" she asked. "I always wanted to try really short hair, but your father would have fussed so. He never wanted me to change anything."

"You look good," he said. "You look happy."

She looked wistful. "I still miss your father terribly, but I'm figuring out how to build a new life on my own. It won't be the same life, but I want it to be a good one."

"You deserve that, Mom."

"I understand you've been busy with other things," she said. "But have you found out anything about my car?"

"We've got a lead on the people responsible for the thefts," he said. "But it's unlikely you'll see your car again. These groups work very fast to get rid of the evidence."

"The officer in Montrose told me the same thing." She sighed. "I talked to my insurance agent and he tells me as soon as they have the police report, he can process the paperwork to cut me a check for the value of the car." She made a face. "Not as much as I paid for it, of course. I can almost hear your father, reminding me how much a new car depreciates."

"You can buy another car," Ethan said.

"Yes, but this time I'll find a nice used one. Maybe that won't be so attractive to thieves."

"Used cars get stolen, too," Ethan said. "Buy a new car if that's what you want."

"Whatever I decide, maybe you'd like to help me pick it out."

Ethan put his hand on her shoulder. "It's your car, Mom. You should pick it out."

She smiled, clearly pleased. "You don't have to worry about me, son." She turned and looked through the glass as Michelle cradled her son, who smiled up at her, waving his hands.

"Look how happy he is to see her," Nancy said. "I would have been beside myself with worry if something like that had happened to you when you were a baby."

"It's good to be part of a happy ending,"

Ethan said. "In my job things don't always work out that way."

He studied Michelle, thinking she had never looked more beautiful than she did now, the lines of tension having vanished from her face, a broad smile softening her face, making her look younger and more open. "For a real happy ending, you have to finish the job," his mom said.

He pulled his gaze away from the mother and baby. "What do you mean?"

Nancy nodded to Michelle. "Have you told her that you love her?"

He didn't ask how his mother knew his feelings. She had always been able to read him; maybe that was something all mothers did. "I don't want to scare her off," he said.

"And you think saying nothing is the way to encourage her to stick around?"

He shoved his hands in his pockets. "She's been through a lot, Mom. I don't want to rush her."

His mom shook her head. "You are so like your father."

"What do you mean?"

"Did you know he never proposed to me? I had to ask him."

"I never knew that." He didn't know much

about his parents' courtship. He had never given it much thought.

"Don't pass up a chance for happiness," she said. "Your problem is that you worry too much about other people—about me, about Michelle, even. Think of yourself for once. Tell her how you feel."

"Yeah, I should do that."

Nancy put on her best mom-lecture face. "If you can face down armed men who want to kill you, you ought to be able to speak honestly with the woman you love," she said.

"You'd think." But sometimes talking about his feelings—especially when so much was on the line—felt a lot riskier than facing a madman with a gun.

MICHELLE COULDN'T GET enough of holding Hunter, or breathing in his scent, or taking in his smile, feeling his little fingers wrap around hers, or seeing the love in his eyes when he looked at her. She felt whole again. Strong again.

Footsteps on the tile hospital floors made her turn to see Ethan walking toward her. "Thank you again," she said. "For everything."

He didn't return her smile—in fact, his expression was serious. "You know this isn't over yet," he said. "Not until we've found Daniel Metwater and put him behind bars."

"Will you put him behind bars when you find him?" she asked.

"We have plenty of evidence to hold him now—his attempt on your life and mine, his link to the kidnappers. I think we can even connect him to the auto thefts in the area, through the Smith brothers. And while we're building our case against him, we'll keep looking for your sister's locket and any other ties we can find between Daniel and David's crimes. He won't get out this time. But until we have him, he's still a danger to you and Hunter."

"I know." She looked down again at the child in her arms. "We'll have to be on our guard, but I think he's running now. I think—or at least I hope—he won't waste time coming after me again."

"You'll need protection until we find him," Ethan said.

She gave him a sideways look, unsure how to interpret the words. "You mentioned something about a safe house."

"I was thinking of something a little different." His expression wasn't flirtatious or teasing. In fact, it was almost grim.

"Is something wrong?" she asked.

"You know I wasn't just doing this for you, or because it was my job," he said.

"What do you mean?"

"I'm as selfish as the next guy—I did this for myself. To stay close to you."

She eyed him warily, still not sure what that somber expression meant. Was he going to arrest her or something? "What are you saying?"

He looked away, then back at her. "I'm saying that I love you. And I don't want you to leave. I want you stay here with me."

Her heart leaped, but she struggled to maintain her composure. She couldn't get carried away. "Are you asking me to move in with you?"

"I'm asking you to marry me. Though I'll take moving in with me, if you want to try that first."

She shook her head.

She almost felt sorry for him, he looked so bereft.

"Are you saying no?"

"I'm saying no, I don't want to start with moving in." She took a deep breath. "And I'm saying yes, I will marry you." He was the best thing that had ever happened to her—well, except for Hunter—and she wasn't going to let him get away.

Now came the smile she had been waiting for. "Really?"

"Did you think I would turn you down?" she asked.

"I didn't know what to think. You're so independent—and I like that, I do. But I'm a cop and I know how you feel about cops..."

She silenced him with a kiss on the cheek. "You're not just any cop. You're the man who believed in me when no one else did—the man who made me see I'm strong enough to do anything—I'm even strong enough to give up a little of my independence to be with the man who means the world to me."

"I always thought I was good at taking care of people," he said. "You've helped me get better at letting them take care of themselves." He pulled her to him and kissed her, long and hard.

She laid her head on his shoulder. "I love you, Ethan Reynolds," she said.

"I love you, Michelle Munson." He stroked the cheek of the baby between them. "And I'll love Hunter, too. I want to be there for him the way my dad was for me."

"You'll be a great dad. And I think you'll make a pretty good husband, too."

"I figure if I mess up, you can keep me in line," he said.

"Hush and kiss me."

"Yes, ma'am."

* * * * *

Look for the next book in Cindi Myers's
THE RANGER BRIGADE:
FAMILY SECRETS *miniseries,*
STRANDED WITH THE SUSPECT,
available next month.

And don't miss the previous titles in
THE RANGER BRIGADE:
FAMILY SECRETS *series:*

MURDER IN BLACK CANYON
UNDERCOVER HUSBAND
MANHUNT ON MYSTIC MESA
SOLDIER'S PROMISE

Available now from Harlequin Intrigue!

Get 2 Free Books,

Plus 2 Free Gifts—

just for trying the Reader Service!

Get 2 Free Books,
Plus 2 Free Gifts -
just for trying the Reader Service!

STRS17R2